A Turn For Worse

W.R. Barna

PublishAmerica
Baltimore

© 2006 by W.R. Barna.
All rights reserved. No part of this book may be reproduced, stored in a retrieval system or transmitted in any form or by any means without the prior written permission of the publishers, except by a reviewer who may quote brief passages in a review to be printed in a newspaper, magazine or journal.

This book is a work of fiction. All characters, places, and events are of the author's imagination, and any similarities to actual people, places, or events is purely coincidental.

First printing

At the specific preference of the author, PublishAmerica allowed this work to remain exactly as the author intended, verbatim, without editorial input.

ISBN: 1-4241-2368-2
PUBLISHED BY PUBLISHAMERICA, LLLP
www.publishamerica.com
Baltimore

Printed in the United States of America

Dedication

To my wife Theresa who was always there
and To my mother and father Lewis M. and Viola E. Barna,
I wonder what they would say?

Acknowledgments

I would like to thank my son Pastor Paul and his wife Pamela who without their mentoring of this computer and e-mail illiterate author, the loose ends at putting together this jungle of words, would never have been legible.

Also thanks to our friends Roberta and Dan, they never said no.

Last but not in any way least, my daughters Donna, Laurie and Lynn, who without their uniqueness in growing into women, this life long dream of mine would never have been accomplished and realized.

W.R.Barna
Slatington, Pa

Foreword

These writings are about an age-old saying, which states "THINGS CAN'T GET MUCH WORSE". When this saying goes uttered, by any mortal, a little known principle applies. This principle is a guy named WORSE. Worse is a principle that springs into action at the mere sound of "THINGS CAN'T GET MUCH WORSE". He is omni-present. He is all knowing. He exists in homes, yours and mine, on all forms of public transportation, weddings, funerals, gala events, all sporting events, places of business, single bars, Bar Mitzvah's Baptisms, hotels, motels, the Federal Interstate system, factories, and houses of ill repute. He also dwells gleefully in schools, under bridges, on lawns at barbeques and picnics, in marriages, in raising kids, at the dentists and doctors offices, in surgery and mylograms, in x-rays, at your brother-in-laws house, he is also sitting acutely aware in barrios, on rickshaws, the Taj Mahal, the IRS, the White House, Parliament, the Kremlin and last but not least in Disneyland.

WORSE is about three foot seven inches in height, weight seventy-five lbs soaking wet. With a great comb-over on his pate, I call the Silvokian swoop, to cover this he wears a blue Homburg with a yellow feather cocked at a jaunty angle. His favorite mode of attire is a gray sweatsuit with Ketchikan, Alaska scrawled across his scrawny chest. He wears on his little feet untied red PF sneakers over black socks that dangle from his little paunch. He is also fond of smoking an EL Producto Cigar. He also possesses a tiger-eye pinky ring, which he wears on his left pinky. He belches frequently and is afflicted with flatulence. He is also endowed with very large ears in which he can always hear these words "THINGS CAN'T GET MUCH WORSE", from any unsuspecting victim. So Mr. WORSE can handle the exclamations of he who feels the uncontrollable urge to mutter, whisper or scream from his own personal depths of despair. "WORSE" hops into action to show he or she that it certainly can and will get worse, for he will personally see to it that it does for he is also ambidextrous.

So the next time you or your loved ones are moved to the point of saying "YOU KNOW WHAT" remember your new acquaintance, for he will hop into action on your behalf and bring more unhappiness than you thought possible or you can just read this book again to prove that his itinerary is right on schedule.

The Decision

I wallowed awake in the dripping, oppressive humidity of the Great Northeast. I had slept once again in a steam room. I was certain any denizen of the region would recognize the situation.

I dragged myself listlessly down the steps of our three-floor rented townhouse. The central air conditioner, as well as the two window units that I had needed to purchase, were valiantly trying to suck away the water from the air, but actually the only thing they were drying up was my wallet. I was surrounded by machines that were fighting a losing battle to keep from drowning in mid-air. Yet the walls seemed to be closing in on me day by day.

For the thousandth time I remembered my good buddy, Dr. Fred, from whom I had purchased two window air conditioners.

Six months ago the good doctor had moved to California, telling me as he departed that if ever I should get tired of the smelly, smokey, drippy, Northeast he would help me move West. This comforting memory seemed to bring me a weird sense of security. I was not really trapped here. I could get out of this place at will!

With each step I took the conviction grew. I could get away from here anytime I wanted. I didn't have to stand for this life in a mechanical breather. Air was meant to be warm, fresh, and sunny. There was no need for us to stay inside to breathe. We needed to be outdoors, free and natural.

Downstairs at last I granted a not-so-"good morning" to my wife and solemnly pronounced, "I'm getting the hell out of this place forever."

She looked at me just the same way she had looked at me the other five hundred or so times I had delivered this declaration. It was her "so-what-else-is-new?" look.

"No, damn it, this time I really mean it!" I am not reneging on this again. Absolutely not! I am committed. This is it! I'm going!"

Now, in order for you to understand what happened next, you must know the cast of characters. In addition to my wife, I have three beautiful daughters. They have discovered, or I should say have been discovered by, the opposite sex (now, remember this little bit of info for it figures largely in my story). And then there is my son, ten years of age, who completes me as a man by giving me someone to instruct so grandly with all that paternal bullshit. You know, those pearls of wisdom such as: "Never slurp your soup; get a haircut; go to school; and you'll go blind if you masturbate." I am fulfilled.

At the time, I was employed by a national company. They did their best to fill the need for travel that my Hungarian ancestors had handed down from the gypsies to me; I still cannot get this hunger out of me. There must be something to it, but, God, it is awful. I see a bus going, I want to be on it. A jet taking off for unknown places can come as close to the feeling one gets from sex as anything that I have found; and to be flying to places unknown is sheer ecstasy for me. I am a real Rover boy.

I had been keeping in touch with my physician friend, Dr. Fred, reminding him of his promise, Southern California. For at least a month, phone calls, letters, and more phone calls were my way of life. My buddy said, "You will never regret moving to California, no one has." He sent me a round-trip ticket on a 747 to the land of ecstasy. I would be leaving JFK and arriving LAX (Los Angeles International Airport). (Californians are either lazy or clever, they never use the middle letters, just x-ing, Ped-xing, LAX, etc.)

And so my journey began. I would seek employment, a house and happiness. The initial journey was underway and uneventful. I was smug as I pondered what life had been like and what the future would hold for me in Sunny Southern California.

I arrived at LAX to find my friend's accountant waiting for me. His accountant! When he was in the Northeast he kept his financial records in the current issue of JAMA. I knew I had initiated the right move, when his houseboy came and picked up my worn Tourister and loaded it into a 1980 Mercedes! Back East he had driven a very unhealthy Ford, which he kept together with baling wire and spit. If it hadn't been for the Turtle Wax he used, the car would have literally fallen apart. All these changes! And he had been in California exactly six months!

Arriving at his abode I noticed an extravagant home, a new car (a BMW), and one more Mercedes in addition to the one in which I was riding. It was silver, and it went very nicely with the maroon BMW. Dr. Fred was smiling upon my arrival, trying to impress me with all of his newly acquired possessions, including another son. He had impresses me enough when he had sent the round-trip airplane ticket, so it was all for naught on his part. However, I listened half-heartedly and looked attentive as only I can, when I am not really paying any attention at all. This is one of the few things my wife does admit that I do well.

After all the pleasantries were over, I went to my room, Imagine having a house large enough for extra rooms!

I have not mentioned before that my buddy is Oriental. His mother-in-law is staying with them. She was very accommodating that first evening in California, except that she spoke nothing but her native tongue. She smiled constantly, with many gold teeth showing. I used sign language and mouth movements in order to keep up my side of the communications. The houseboy also spoke his native tongue, and nothing else. Oh well, it was only a minor problem. I managed. Dr. Fred's number one son can only be described as a very hyperactive fellow. Peeking into my room at various times, trying to catch me nude was one of his favorite games. I also might add he is overly bright.

The first night and ensuing day went well, save for the smell of frying fish in the morning, a smell that is still in my nostrils. Well, different strokes for different folks. I am liberal.

His wife also appeared different. I recognized Sasson Jeans and saw newly capped teeth. I knew I made the right move so far. "This is great, this is great," I found myself repeating. I telephoned the Little Woman and related what I had seen and heard. In only forty hours my buddy had arranged for a house for us to live in, rent free; and a very promising position with a large business. Dr. Fred told me on the phone that he would not let me starve. Dr. Fred's wife informed the Little Woman of all the great things, material and spiritual, that they have acquired in moving to the "Land of Plenty." The good wife was not too impressed. My male-crazed daughters were not sold on the deal either, but knowing my power of persuasion, I felt this to be the least of my worries.

I was introduced to a smiling, friendly, little man who assured me that my position with his firm was solid, and I was to worry about nothing.

Next, I was whisked to the house that would be mine to live in, rent-free. Since it was rent free, I would not care if it were a chicken coop. I cannot believe it. It was a mile above sea level, with a view overlooking a lake, mountain, and a small airport. I was astounded. The interior of the house was bright orange with redwood ceiling, genuine redwood that someone had toiled to build. I was going to live there rent and mortgage free! I spied the master bedroom, and when a deflated waterbed was pointed out to me, I was ecstatic. I noticed, however, one oddity here, green peacocks were strolling on a silver wall beneath the other redwood ceiling. Now, I'm not one for caring what I live in, but I knew that this would give the Little Woman trouble. Being the charming salesman I was, I figured that I would not have a problem. I also noticed more people in the room than there actually were, but in my excitement, I had failed to notice that the walls were mirrored. I stepped onto the patio to check out how I might look with the scenic background behind me. Just like Steve McQueen, I thought, in that movie with the title that escaped me. Everyone was so happy for me. I was happy, my friends were beaming. I was sold!

After dinner, rice again with some strange purple things, I proudly called home and told the spouse all the wondrous things that we now had, in just ninety-six hours, too. I told her, "Your husband is a real charmer." She still sounded reluctant, but somewhat interested, and asked me questions like: "Does it have curtains?" "I don't know."

"Does it have a dishwasher?" "I don't know."

"Does it have a washer and dryer?" "I don't know."

"Does it have a refrigerator?" "I don't know."

"What about carpeting?" Ahah! This one I knew. "Yes, it does have carpets and they are orange."

"What?" she gasped, "Orange," are you crazy? Well I backed off now. "Not really orange, sort of rust, you know." Just for that I am not going to tell her about the peacocks. Now she asked "shall we sell the washer and dryer, the refrigerator, the dishwasher, etc.?" I replied, trying to disarm her, "Don't worry about it. We will talk about that when I return home." She uncovered this attempt at deception, having know me for twenty years, and wanted to speak with Dr. Fred. He assured her that this was not really important and she, knowing that Dr. Fred would not lie to her, was soothed. Things were moving in a positive direction.

Everything had been accomplished in only five days. I was ready to return to the east and my family, but had to wait two days because I was on a super-saver flight. It would cost Dr. Fred one hundred and eighty dollars more to leave early. Oh well, I could stand two more glorious days in the California sun. Now Dr. Fred and I would have some time to talk and tan.

The arrangements were that I return east. The house would be held for as long as it took me to get to California with my group. My job was solid and would wait for me. This seemed too good to be true. Nothing like this had ever happened to me before. I did not need United's Ocean-to-Ocean Service to fly me to New York. I was so elated I could have flown by flapping my arms and carrying my worn Tourister in my teeth.

The Move

A journey of a thousand miles times three, begins with the very first step. I landed uneventfully at JFK to find my wife and son waiting for me. She was smiling and dressed beautifully. That was new. I had landed scores of times before and had only seen a stranger with coils of wire coming out of her head. I hugged and kissed her, and hugged and kissed my little boy who immediately said "I am not going to California." I had held back my ace in the hole for him. When I explained that there was a large real fishpond built in on the patio of the new house, he was immediately sold. "That was easy," I thought. "What a salesman!" By the time we were on the George Washington Bridge my little boy could not wait to go. One problem solved. The Little Woman was getting less reluctant, too. By the time we arrived home, a drive of seventy miles, she was moderately interested. This was the state of things on October tenth, 1980.

Arriving back home I found my two male-crazed daughters. The elder of the two spoke, "I don't want to hear anything about moving to California." A minor problem, I figured. Hah! The younger girl did not speak, but looked away from me every time I tried to direct the conversation back to the Land of Golden Opportunity. I also noticed a new male addition to our family in the person of Joseph J. Vaughan, who was handsome, dark and tall. He was our youngest latest love. A passing thing, I felt, or as my mother used to call it, "puppy love." Joseph was smiling, but apparently afraid of talking. I found out later that he was a local jock, for whom every girl in town just couldn't wait to lay her body down. And he was in my house, courting daughter number three. She is blond, blue-eyed and beautiful. She would not speak to me about anything at all, much less about moving to California. My trained eye watched as they melted toward the front door to say their goodnights. Oh, those two beautiful dolls, the one is blue-eyed and slick as deer guts on a doorknob; and the other brown-haired, dark-eyed, beautiful and smart as they come.

Enter the oldest daughter, who is a whirling dervish, likened sometimes also to the Tasmanian devil. We exchanged pleasantries after I succeeded in stopping her long enough to say hello. She was in the house but two minutes, and a catastrophe took place. It seems daughter number three has grown enough to fit into daughter number one's jeans, and was at this very moment wearing them. An argument ensued and lasted until mother stepped forward and stopped the brawl. The house was calm until eldest daughter found, of all things, a "zit" on her chin. This was good for another half-hour of abrasiveness on her part. This, definitely, was not the time for selling California to the group. I passed for the evening, and enjoyed pleasant dreams of a movie contract, the sun, Disneyland, and work, in that order.

The next few weeks were a blur of activity, parts of which were listening to crying daughters. Seems two were in love, and the other was concerned about her career as a nuclear physicist and losing all of her dear friends. She kept repeating, "I don't want to hear anything about moving to California." Daughter number three was screaming about my breaking her heart, and about how thoughtless I was to talk of moving. "I hate California," she kept saying over and over. And all the while I recalled all of them crying, just two years before, when we had left California for home from a vacation. Things change, I supposed.

Now, amid all of the outcries comparing me to an SS Storm Trooper, I pushed on making arrangements for the departure. First, I called the moving companies and decided on one. The representative set an appointment time and, surprisingly, kept it right to the minute.

The October sun was particularly bright that afternoon when the man, in the person of Mr. Thomas A. Felmer, arrived. Mr. Felmer (call me Tom) was tall, gentle, and a very trustworthy fellow, I thought. I had a total of forty-two hundred dollars. Call me Tom calculated forty-seven hundred pounds of furniture. He assured me that the couch does weigh two hundred-fifty pounds and estimated the move to cost three thousand three hundred dollars.

Hmmm, quick calculations told me I either had to burn some furniture or unload some junk. So, unload the junk we did. The bats from Bat Day at the Phillies-Padres game went, along with my old sports magazines (at least 100 pounds worth). Pounds of old clothes went to the Salvation Army. The daughters were not giving up anything I mean nothing. Dear old Dad was not getting much cooperation in his pursuit of happiness. We still had four thousand pounds of furniture. The cost was now only three thousand, which left me a grand total of one thousand two hundred dollars to my name, and we hadn't left yet. At this point, I was declared legally insane, by my wife. But I could see the palms swaying gently and feel my skin a glowing gold, so on I pushed. Daughter number two was still insistent, "I don't want to hear about moving to California."

The target date was now only two weeks away. On November fourteenth, 1980, the family was scheduled to head west.

Now, moving four thousand pounds of furniture takes quite a bit of doing. The movers arrived on November tenth. Note how I left three days for whittling down what each one wanted to keep. I could compare this to the pile of rubbish that was left, and try in my mind's eye, reduce it only to what would fit in to the trunk of a sedan, and a small hatchback.

The movers came, bringing the lamp-wrapping ladies. "Never broke one yet." They packed, carted, carried, crated, lumbered, swore, and dragged all of our life into that big cold white, and blue van. Now, remembering my finances, I broke the news (after the van was loaded, of course) that I would like the furniture to remain in storage until I called for it. Mr. Mover sort of looked at me as though I had just hijacked his truck, and said, "What the hell is going on here?" and demanded the telephone to call his office. The conversation went something like this:

Mr. Mover: "Yea, that's what he said!"
Unknown voice...
Mr. Mover: Well what the hell do I do now?"
Unknown voice...
Mr. Mover: "I'm supposed to be in Nashville on the fifteenth, and this joker's furniture is on the truck!"
Unknown voice...
Mr. Mover: "Yea, OK, here he is...Hey-she wants to talk to you!"
Me: "Hello..."
Unknown voice: "What are you trying to do here (no more sirs) Mister?"
Me: "Nothing, Ma'am, just changed my mind. I would appreciate your accommodating me. I am sorry for any inconvenience I have caused you."
Unknown voice: "This means a whole change of paperwork, setting up storage space; and it will cost you more. Do you realize this?"

Of course, I realized this. I thought, "All I am seeing at this point is shedding walnuts and oak trees, and a cold wind blowing through our open door, instead of me in California, and with about four hundred dollars left after traveling across the U.S.A." But, comforted by Dr. Fred's words, "We will not let you starve," I heard myself speaking, "I beg you please to understand my position. I do not know if the house we are moving to will accommodate all my furniture. I will have to solve this problem when I get there."

After bantering back and forth for a half-hour, she finally agreed upon storage. Now, remember this for future reference.

The Little Woman and daughter three were shrieking, and had decided to have me committed on the spot. I was still pursuing the golden west, most frantically now. I was so close I just couldn't lose it now. The van left with my furniture down the cold November highway, and I walked back into our townhouse, empty save for five people staring at me for direction and guidance, in a manner that I hadn't seen since they all were in diapers.

My first command was that they take everything in the house and place it in the living room so I could decide if it would fit into our cars. "What's left?" I bark. "Where did that come from?" Hmmm. "You mean the movers didn't take that? What are we going to do with all this stuff?" What was left was not going to fit into the sedan and number one daughter's hatchback, the Little Woman insisted. Being the dreamer, I said, "No problem." It was now two days to D-day (departure day, not to be confused with the other one, the Allied invasion of Normandy, although it was shaping up to be just about as monumental). I now resorted to my strong point—calling friends— anyone—asking if they knew someone who needed a sixteen inch" Sharp TV that didn't work or a giant five-foot rabbit that daughter number one hid from the movers. She insisted on taking it in her car on our trek to Southern California.

I managed to peddle off some merchandise and realize some cash, but the Little Woman still insisted that the remaining items would never fit. Needless to say, we were sleeping on the floor for the second night, and the telephone had been disconnected. Pure peace it was, with but a twinge of anxiety.

I had noticed, but not with any great interest, that handsome Jock and Burly Curly, the latter being number one daughter's beau, were getting greener and paler by the day, and sending me looks that gave me a chill when I looked into their dark young eyes. The best explanation would be they would like to kill me. But I pursued my quest for that easy, golden life in you-know-where.

Much of this time between my return from California and D-day, friends had taken us to dinner and invited us for going-away parties. Free meals and true compassion from people we sometimes did not even know that well. You cannot bear a three thousand mile move. The hoopla was over, the moving van had gone and most of the good-byes were said. Daughter number two was still insisting: "I don't want to hear anything about moving to California." Daughter number one was still not going, and daughter number three kept insisting her life was ruined and that she would not go. I had to think quickly. I promised I would fly them back for Christmas. Where I was going to get the money, I didn't know. One thing about me, however, I do what I say.

Now, I am not one to believe in omens or hints of impending disaster, but a few things happened two days before D-day that caused such thoughts to pass through my thick skill for a fleeting moment. Maybe someone was trying to tell me something. The pile on the living room floor wouldn't fit into the mode of transportation we wanted to use, to leave this Godforsaken, humid-in-summer, cold-and-damp-in-winter, north east. After much sweating, and pushing stuff into nooks and crannies in the cars, moving and removing our possessions, we still wound up with an overload that was too valuable to throw away or sell. It would have to be left with my mother and my very reluctant mother in law a real sweetheart to the end.

As we deposited these various items just one day before D-day, a very light snow started falling. It was really beautiful! I remember thinking that because I would never have to contend with that again. At that moment I was descending a set of stairs that I usually could go down blindfolded and backwards, when I felt a sharp pain in my ankle. It twisted and snapped back. I heard no crack, but I was suddenly flat on my ass in the lovely snow that I just though would never give me trouble again. Within an hour my foot was black.

I asked the Little Woman to call her friend, Sally, a not a bad bone in her body very capable nurse. I hobbled to the car, and we drove to her house. She looked and said it might or might not be broken. Only an x-ray would tell the true tale. Since I had quit my job and had no hospitalization, this idea was put to rest. I was guarding my cash with my life. I made the mistake of asking Sally, "What's the worst possible effect this could have on my driving three thousand miles?" Her reply was anything but positive, as she went into multiple medical terms. The gist of her answer was that I could possibly become a cripple from a not-so-good supply of blood in my already swollen foot. My skull was getting thicker by the moment with a desire so strong for California that I replied I would risk having my foot cut off, as long as I could get to the Promise Land. My woman was thinking about commitment AGAIN. In fact, I thought I saw her make a move for the phone.

On I pushed. The light snow that was falling was now heavy, six inches deep. The next day was D-day and now we had no home to go to. We had returned the key to the superintendent of the townhouse in which we had lived for the last eight years. Before my fall, I had asked my mother, who was going to make the trek with us, if we could sleep at her house the last night. I felt it only proper and nostalgic that I should spend the last night in the northeast in the house in which I had grown up. A sentimentalist to the end. We drove, car loaded, ankle swollen, my wife mumbling, to spend what was not to be my last night in the northeast.

Now, I know the power of prayer is STRONG, but obviously the Deity listens to teenage girls and super jock teenage boys before He listens to a thirty-nine-year-old idealist. We awoke to blizzard conditions. The wind chill factor was minus twenty degrees Fahrenheit, with fourteen inches of white and brown snow. Upon looking out the window on D-day I muttered, "Bullshit!", and resigned myself to the fact that this was not the day to pioneer. Super jock and Burly Curly appeared at seven a.m. No school for these guys today. They were spending the day with my male-crazed daughters, who were thankful for the twenty-four-hour reprieve and still not saying a word to dear old Dad. They still looked at me with gazes that made me want to take cover for the day. Super jock did speak. He said, "I hope it snows for a month." I gave him a caustic look, but he looked back more caustically; and I figured since he was five inches taller, and forty pounds heavier, and twenty years younger, I had better stop with the caustic glares. The day was spent with Super jock and daughter number three, and Burly Curly and daughter number one frolicking in the snow and making me feel more guilty by the moment.

My ankle and foot did not even resemble an ankle or a foot. I did not complain, however, for I had reached the point of no return. No house, no job, the furniture God only knows where (perhaps Nashville), but I was still intoxicated with thoughts of swaying palms, movie contracts, golden sun, and work, in that at order.

Now I should explain why my seventy-six-year-old mother was foolish enough to take this trip. She had an old friend in Ventura, California. Mother fears flying, so plans were for her to stay at the old friend's house for one month, and fly back with daughters number one, two and three as I had promised. The true reason, I think, was that she figured I was insane and wanted to be there when her youngest son was committed.

The day dragged on. The Little Woman finally realized that her crazed husband was really going to do this, and I saw in her face a look that said, "He has pulled some ridiculous stunts, but this one is a real beaut." I felt, at this point, that no one had really taken me seriously until now. I was muttering under my breath, "Ain't no way that I'm returning to this rancid dump ever again." I learned later never to say "never" or "ever."

As my love affair with this mistress three thousand miles away continued, it now became a challenge of absurd proportions. If no one else was going, I was prepared to walk. I made a phone call to Dr. Fred; and, of course, I got his answering service. This boy must really be rolling in dough! I now have six phone numbers to try to contact him. He called back, laughed when he heard that it was snowing and said very reassuringly, "We will be waiting for you when you arrive." I felt good again and confident.

The Little Woman was on the telephone a good part of the day talking to various friends and doing a lot of whispering, with cupped hands, into the mouthpiece. My paranoia was not running, it was galloping. But all this blinded me, I still could see was swaying palms, movie contracts, and golden sun. We'll think about work when we get there.

Super jock and Curly Burly were finally realizing that they had ten hours left. I had disclosed that seven thirty am was to be lift off. Not seven thirty one am, nor seven twenty nine am, but seven thirty am sharp. "Everyone get that message." I was a mountain of strength now. I must have spoken Arabic because no one answered, they just stared. My number one son mumbled an audible affirmative. He must understand Arabic. To bed early, for early to bed and early to rise makes a man wealthy, wise and healthy—or is it the other way around? It did not matter. I was high on everything. Even the most severe looks form Super jock and Burly Curly and my lovely family could not affect me. I was on a roll. I dreamed of beaches, palms, movie contracts, golden sun, and maybe employment.

I was startled awake by the mangy she-hound my mother had acquired since my father's death. At five am, the dog was barking sharply and constantly. I knew something must be wrong. The wrong was Super jock sleeping in his car. Said car was a brown concoction of nuts and bolts that ran it and still runs to this day, much to everyone's surprise, including his own. He was huddled not unlike Washington's troops at Valley Forge, and was scantily clad, and on the verge of frostbite from exposure. His love for daughter number three was strong and enduring. It had to be, to do that. He said later that he had arrived at four a.m. because he figured I might have had thoughts of sneaking out on him at five a.m. Talk about paranoia!!

Enter Burly Curly who was just as cold in his Adidas sneakers and dungarees and the cutoff sweatshirt he always knew made me jealous of his biceps. (Compared to his, I don't have any). They both had the look of wounded fawns. I almost gave way to tears; with one hour to go I knew I had better stay our of their way. I had read a story about wounded animals, and it said they are very dangerous at this time and can inflict untold wounds.

Time to pile into the cars. It was eight forty five am before I could drag daughter's number one and three from the back yard where everyone was crying. It was difficult to wrestle them from the clutches of the two wounded fawns. Daughter number two was still saying, "I don't want to hear anything about moving to California." My number one son was asking about and planning on the types of fish he would put into the pond of our rent-free, mortgage-free home. The Little Woman, seeing that I could not be dissuaded from this venture, started to organize the mob. My mother's hound was barking, the girls were crying, Super jock and Burly Curly were cursing me openly now. We must go, for I could almost feel the sting from their punches and kicks.

We were in the car at last. Number one son, the Little Woman, and my mother and I were in the sedan. Number one, two and three daughters, were in the hatchback. I wondered about two stowaways, so I checked one more time and was convinced that the way the car was packed no one could have possibly been in there, much less Super jock and Burly Curly. I noticed a giant white rabbit in the car, and I thought of Jimmy Stewart in "Harvey." For a moment I was convinced I had snapped. It was just Burly Curly's "Remember-me-always" present, which daughter number one had assured me, weeks ago, she had given back. We were gassed up and ready to go. Upon leaving the service station, I noticed the brown concoction of nuts and bolts following us, not too closely, but close enough. I accelerated and lost them in the traffic. I did not look back until I was on the Pennsylvania Turnpike headed west, and I looked to see if the blue hatchback was there. The only car I would see in the rear view mirror for the next six days and five nights, to my surprise, was there.

California Here We Come

The rolling hills of Pennsylvania finally gave way, after five and one-half hours; to the old tough lady know as Wheeling, West Virginia. On and on we drove, to our first overnight stop at Reynoldsburg, Ohio. It was west of home, but not far enough west for me. We had settled into the room and had eaten, when, I couldn't believe my ears, the telephone rang. Now, no one in the universe could possibly have known where we were. Unknown to me at the time, it was the beginning of Super jock's, Curly Burly's and my contribution to the stockholders of Ma Bell. It seems that daughter number three had called Super jock upon arrival at the Holiday Inn and given him the phone number, as did daughter number one, who let Burly Curly have our new twelve-hour-old address and number.

Now these two have trouble remembering the alphabet, but I am sure the phone numbers of every Holiday Inn, Ramada and Hilton was and is forever burned into their seventeen and eighteen-year-old brains. I announced that again we were leaving early in the a.m., cleverly not giving a time for fear of being embarrassed again. At twelve thirty am EST the phone was jingling off the hook and daughter number three was at the phone before I could open the other eye and heard, "I miss you too."

"How can this be?" I thought. It was not even eighteen hours from departure.

The next day dawned cold and snowy, although the interstate was free of snow. We motored through Ohio, and into Indianapolis, Indiana, where we stopped for lunch and gasoline. Daughters one and three dashed to any pay phone available to reach out and touch someone at any stop, keeping Super jock and Burly Curly well posted on our progress. Being fairly good at reading lips, I noticed the word love being formed quite a bit. I mentioned this to the Little Woman and she shrugged, and both she and mother agreed, "Puppy love." I did not quite feel this way because while we were stopped at McDonald's for lunch, I noticed that daughters one, two and three made certain to camp as far away from me as possible. Daughter number three had a golden, ruby-colored class ring tucked into her little bosom, and she is clutching it for dear life. I was unaware that she had this trinket, as was the Little Woman.

Into the flat lands of Illinois and on into Missouri we went. We laid our burdens down for the night. I could not look into any mirror without seeing a blue hatchback. This can become quite difficult when shaving. Settling in for the evening, they now insisted upon separate rooms. "It will cost too much money," I declared. Daughters number one, two, and three declared just as strongly, in unison, "We're not staying in the same room, after you have ruined our lives." I submitted, overcome by guilt. I did hear the phone ringing in the next room several times that evening.

Heading directly west into Independence, Missouri, I told the girls that we were stopping at the Harry S. Truman Library, because I have great admiration for him as a man and President. I do not admire many people as I do this man. I made a men's room stop at the Harry S. Truman Library, and read over the urinal a noteworthy message, "While you're reading this sign, you're pissing on your shoes." I guess even great Presidents are not exempt from some form of degradation. When I returned, daughters number one, two and three flatly stated that no way were they going to a dead President's Library. They would be happy to find a shopping center in

Independence to while away the several hours. Now you may say, this man is crazy, leaving three daughters loose on their own. They could very well start heading east. I thought of that, believe me, but as I mentioned before, I am not one of those of little faith and I do know my offspring. I told them, "Meet us here in two hours." Daughter number one said, "OK." And off they went to the nearest pay phone and that unknown shopping center. I know daughter number one had all of the instincts of a radar tower when it comes to directions. She could find a JCPenny's in the Gobi Desert in a sandstorm. I knew she would find the way back to Harry's library in the allotted time.

It was a very pleasurable stop. Because it was November, not many people were sightseeing. I was enthralled by Mr. Truman's recorded voice telling me all about his office, and the many artifacts, pens and pencils, doodles, papers, and globes belonging to this great American. I saw the sign "The Buck Stops Here," and was truly impressed. I realized then what I had admired about this man. He was honest and responsible. After more gazing at Mr. Truman's grave and the beautiful setting, we concluded our tour. Lo and behold, daughters number one, two and three were waiting for us on the steps of the library. I did notice a slight indentation of a phone in my daughter number three's ear, and her hand was somewhat curved as though it were still clutching a phone.

Off we went, heading west through Kansas City and Topeka, just making Hays, Kansas on very little gasoline. I was becoming more and more reluctant to shell out close to one dollar and sixty cents per gallon for the pink gold. Again, getting separate rooms, we laid our heads to rest in Hays, Kansas, and found out who shot J.R.

Onward we drove into Colorado, and my mother was becoming noticeably agitated at the sight of the majestic snow-covered Rockies. As we neared Denver, I don't think my mother quite believed that we were to travel over those high peaks and through that rugged country. I told her that there was no other way to the golden land except over those mountains. I noticed in mother's eyes that the slight anxiety noted earlier, was now becoming stark fear as we traveled up 5,000, 6,000, 8,140 feet. It had begun snowing and my mother was visibly shaken. I was trying to keep the blue hatchback in my rear view mirror. Up 9,200, 10,320 feet, Eisenhower Pass is at 11,000 feet and it was still snowing. The blue hatchback was still there, but sliding. Cinders were bouncing off the windshield as we slid into Vail, where we slept amongst the purple and white Rocky Mountains, and paid a record one dollar and sixty nine point nine cents per gallon for gas. We ate dinner in our usual manner—number one son, the Little Woman, my mother and I in one booth; and, about four booths away, were daughters number one, two, and three. The check, however, always found its way back to my table.

The next day, we were driving off Route seventy, through little towns and hamlets in Utah, when a monstrous snowstorm was advancing right behind us. I was trying to beat this storm, and it was proving a real challenge. I knew that to get caught in this rugged country could be at best overwhelming. My mother, at this point, could be described as frantic. The clouds were moving fast; and of course, our man on the radio wasn't helping mother's condition at all. Every time he came on with the weather report, I burst into song, but there is not a man alive who can fool his mother or his wife. I finally pulled into a motel, in southwest Utah, ready to ride out the storm. The Little Woman became very vocal about the proprietor's habits. He seemed to grab his crotch quite frequently and pick his ass with his free hand at the same time. She informed me that she wouldn't stay here if he threw in a free Cadillac with the night's stay. I tried to explain that anything was better than getting caught on that interstate in the snow, with the next town sixty-three miles away. I didn't care if he picked his ass, crotch and nose at the same time, I was going to stand my ground this time, so there. "We are staying here for the night."

Five minutes later, we were back on the interstate looking for a motel. I was trying to find out how far we were from Cedar City, Utah. There was dead silence in the car. It took three hours to drive the sixty miles before we pulled into our resting place for the evening. My anxiety level had attained new heights from the drive, the blizzard conditions, and watching for the little blue hatchback in the mirror. I was as nervous and anxious as I have ever been. We all ate in silence, together this time. Daughters number one, two and three must have had a twinge of anxiety also. The check didn't have far to go; it stayed local.

I realized. Upon awakening to a foot and half of snow, that I had given away or left all my winter clothes back east. I felt surely that I wouldn't need gloves or boots in Southern California. I was now freezing my ass off, getting the snow off each car with a Holiday Inn brochure while everyone else waited in the room until it was clear, and I said, "Let's go."

We stopped to fill the tanks, and by now I was gasoline shopping. I didn't care what I put in that tank as long as it burned. I saw a gas sign at one dollar and thirty-eight cents per gallon, so I pulled in. Too late, he had the hose in the tank and was filling up at one dollar and fifty-nine cents per gallon. I said, "Hey, how about that?"—Pointing to the one dollar thirty eight sign. The gas man explained that he didn't have any more numbers, so he had just left the sign as is. I was not going to make a scene. He then interjected, "Going to California?" "Yes," I said proudly. His expression told me that he had seen many, many people before making this trek with an eastern temporary license plate on. I didn't like the way he asked. (Oh, what the hell, just fill the two cars up and let's go.) The California border, by my calculations couldn't be but four to five hours from here. Oh, sweet glorious land of opportunity, here I come! He also mentioned that it would be clear sailing after forty miles on the interstate. "Must be the sun's reflection from California," I said cleverly. No one laughed but me.

Old gasman was right. Forty miles down the road it was clear as a bell, sun shining, highway clear, not even slush. Some snow was on the mountain peaks, and with the sun shining it was a beautiful sight to behold.

Now, on our final assault, I noticed there was a small tip of Arizona we must pass through. From my experience Arizona and Indians are synonymous. "Let's see if we can find Chief Crazy Horse's brother," I said. Well, I didn't find his brother, but I must have found his cousin. We stopped at a little adobe restaurant. On the way out I noticed a drunken Indian rocking on the porch with his squaw. The squaw was saying nothing, but spitting in his face every twenty seconds or so, and this wasn't bothering the chief at all. I tried not to look as number one son said, "Look, Dad." I whispered, "I see, sshhh." By this time, chief wobbled to his feet and barked, "Hey, white man, Hey, white man." I looked, and he was waving back and forth. The squaw was still spitting at an imaginary chief. We stood but fifteen feet apart. I went over, out of courtesy, telling my number one son to get the hell out of here. (If you don't know by now that I am adventurous or crazy, you wasted your money on this book.) He clasped my hand in a vise-like grip and bellowed, "I never met a white man from Pennsylvania." He had noticed my temporary tag and proceeded to tell me of his very impressive war record. What the good old U.S.A. had done to him and his brothers, and how they had gotten their Asses kicked on Iwo Jima. Now, I understood his frustrations and aggressiveness, but just when I felt empathy for him, he screwed it all up by saying, "You bastard white man from Pennsylvania, remember you're in my fucking country now, and don't you ever forget it." (I don't believe he was code talking at this point.) I was still locked in his vise-like clasp and I couldn't figure a way out without a real fracas.

The good Lord has endowed me with many talents, but holding my own in a brawl with a half-crazed, drunken Indian was not one of them. This guy wasn't letting go. I said, "You're right, Chief, you're right. I don't belong in this country. This is yours, and I'll be leaving it as soon as you let me. I can't leave if you don't let me go, now, can I?"

The squaw was still spitting and giggling, and three or four other braves had gathered. He looked at me with steely eyes, debating whether I was worth kicking the shit out of, and then said, "Goodbye," and released me.

I walked a very fast pace back to the car, still shaking, with my heart playing the Minute Waltz in twenty seconds, and got the hell out of there. The Little Woman asks, "What was going on?" I swallowed hard and said "Oh, nothing. Just some guy telling me war stories." The speedometer did not get below eighty until I saw "Welcome to Nevada." We stopped in the first casino we saw, as I had promised my mother, against the Little Woman's wishes.

To know my mother is to know true humility—kind, loving, and giving; but a tremendous addiction to the slots. She can pump nickels and quarters into those babies faster than they can take them. She would not leave this slot machine, or any slot machine for that matter. I saw a situation developing where it might take Patton's army to get her out of here. I could smell the good land, and was starting to see California plates and that only wetted my appetite for my new home. I bartered, begged, cajoled, and finally onward we went, closer to my fantasy. We were approaching Las Vegas, and I was hoping devoutly that my mother might miss it. But she casually remarked, "Isn't this Las Vegas?" "Yes, it is, Mom; but, it's going to be a real mess with that MGM fire last week and all that." But my mother is a very bright woman, and we traded off for the last town in Nevada for her to gamble again. It was a gem of place called "Pop's Oasis." Mother's affair with the slots did not last quite so long, but I have known her to forsake eating for those one-armed bandits.

We were now twenty-seven miles from California's border—fifteen miles—nine miles—six miles— "There it is!" I shrieked; "Welcome to California!" I motioned to the little blue hatchback. I was making motions with my hands and rocking back and forth by myself, and all the Little Woman said was, "It looks just as dirty and brown as it did before." I didn't care, I was close to heaven, pointing out everything and anything from the desert blooming, to the helicopters overhead for our safety. I continued to talk to myself for the next one hundred fifty miles or so to Barstow, where the McDonald's that looks like a train appeared, and we stopped. I was exultant and insisted that we have our dinner here, in the McDonald's that looks like a railroad car. "Clever Californians," I simpered. "Who else would think of something like this?" No one was impressed but me.

Upon leaving the little blue hatchback, daughter number one squinted, and I noticed everyone else was squinting. I, with my eastern trying-to-look-western sunglasses on, was very cool. No one else was, for they were bitching about the heat. "The heat!", I exclaimed. "We just left five days and a lifetime of slop." The temperature was a moderate seventy-five degrees, and it was one week before Thanksgiving.

The California sun was already starting to tan my pale face and arms, I was positive. So I shed my V-neck sweater and thought seriously about taking my shoes off. The Little Woman just shot me a look, which told me she would rather be anywhere but here. Little did I know that everything, every situation, every breath, every conversation, all that is connected with survival would, and could, be compared, from this moment on, to climbing Mount Rainier with Vans on, and a two-hundred-pound knapsack on my tanned back. It's a very good thing that the good Lord in His infinite wisdom allows you to exercise your free will without letting you know what's in store for you. This was the beginning of nineteen months of aggravation, high anxiety, open cursing and disharmony the likes of which I have never seen. Frustrating, horrendous situations; ridiculous, unbelievably taxing and frightening events became our daily lot. I assure you now that every event, situation, place and circumstance, could possibly be true!

The High Price of Rent Free Housing

We ate in McDonald's that looks like a railroad car with our usual seating arrangements. The daughters three were several booths away. They were becoming farther apart from me once more. In a little while we were back on the road again.

On I-fifteen I saw the first real signal of enchantment, "Los Angeles, eighty-four miles." Passing through Victorville, I ventured, "What a quaint desert town." No reply from the Little Woman. On through the desert and mountains we drove, and I was starting to notice a black cloud of something in the sky. I paid no attention; but at this point, if I had possessed an ounce of foresight or believed in omens, I would have headed east or north or south— anywhere but west. But the skull was thicker than ever, and on I traveled with the little blue hatchback, bearing the great white rabbit sitting stoically, with my three daughters. They were following the bronze sedan trustingly into the mountains of San Bernardino.

Our little black cloud now became a giant black cloud, and the radioman, on the airways, was starting to get very jumpy explaining that the combined situation of the dry weather and the Santa Annas (What the hell is the Santa Annas anyway?) was causing a very large fire. They were diverting traffic off the San Berdoo Freeway to the Foothill Freeway. It was three P.M., and if the Little Woman hadn't assured me that it was, I would have bet everything I could, that it was three AM. not three PM because it was as black as night. Our man on the airways was sounding quite upset and was making remarks about hundreds being told to leave their homes in San Berdoo. (I was to find out later that "San Berdoo" is the California version of San Bernardino. As I mentioned before, they are either clever or lazy.) Twenty minutes later he was screaming over the airway that the fire was shaping up to be the largest fire in Southern California in twenty years. You guessed it! Who was smack-dab in the middle of it, but the rover and his clan. What timing! It could happen to very few.

However, I still was drugged by movie contracts, the golden sun, which was now totally gone, and swaying palms, which I could not even see, and fame, which was almost turning to survival. I could not see the blue hatchback with my offspring and the great white rabbit sitting stoically in the back. Dark ash was snowing all around us, and the radioman was now talking about thousands being evacuated, and we were stopped by the CHIPS (California Highway Patrol). We were diverted to the Foothill Freeway. My sense of direction, at best, on a clear, sunny day, is poor; and now I was about to approach the most complicated freeway system in the nation. The visibility was as far as the ornament on the hood of the sedan. I anxiously screamed at the Little Woman to get the map of Southern California.

Plans had dictated that mother go to Ventura to stay with her old friend and that we drive back to stay with Dr. Fred. The best laid plans of mice and men—HA…We drove on for one hour through names like Rialto, Colton, Ontario, (I thought that was in Canada), Upland, Claremont, Monclair, LaVerne and the town where we were going to live, San Dimas. (I was told later the town was named for one of the thieves that died on the cross with Jesus.) I noticed a sign through the lifting ash and smoke that told me the 210 Freeway was near, and I recalled this freeway from my initial journey. I knew that this freeway goes west, and Ventura is west.

Visibility had returned to the point that I could put my sunglasses back on. I was pleased with that for, again, I looked like a native, except for those temporary eastern tags. I could see the little blue hatchback in the mirror again. I looked up and saw a house on the mountain, and I told the Little Woman with confidence, "There it is." She pointed to the house for our offspring's benefit; but, of course, they had no idea what she was doing. Daughter number one interpreted this to mean we were exiting the freeway. It took forty-five minutes to find them again. Later, I found that I had been confused and that was not our house at all. So, for my not knowing what the hell I was talking about, it cost us forty-five minutes of valuable daylight, which would have come in very handy later.

We still had about fifty miles or so to go to Ventura, and it was now approaching nightfall, and we were coming to Pasadena and the Rose Bowl sign. I then encountered what can only be described as one huge used car lot and parking garage...this was the Ventura Freeway. There were little cars, big cars, fast ones, slow ones, expensive ones, not-so-expensive ones, lifted-in-the-rear ones, and lifted-in-the-front ones. We were thrust into this without so much as a single word of warning.

Our land speed went from sixty-five mph to zero in about eleven seconds. The way these myriad chunks of steel were going into exits or coming onto the freeway, I could not distinguish our little blue hatchback from the hundreds of similar cars. I reluctantly took off my shades, for it was now dark. Daughters number one, two, and three and the great white rabbit were invisible. They had no idea where old friend's place was, and, to be quite frank, neither did I. Daughter number one amazed me, for she was fighting for her life, weaving, cutting off, and squeezing to try and stay at least five cars back. I had no idea where they were, and I was praying aloud now. Mother was afraid of never seeing her grandchildren again; and my Little Woman, who is by nature a very cool lady, was losing her composure at the thought of never seeing her first, second and third-born anymore. I, being not so cool, was hyperventilating. I instructed number one son to lie on the top of the back seat and keep his eye out for anything that looked as though it even remotely resembled them.

The situation was worsening by the second, with more and more cars coming on and going off, cutting in and squeezing out, and tapping bumpers. Five full lanes of American, Japanese, German,

and homemade metals jockeying for position and flipping me off—
another famous pastime of freeway drivers. They were all grinding to
one gigantic halt; flowing and slowing from speeds of sixty mph to
zero in nothing flat. At this point I was sure of two things; being
overrun by the large eighteen-wheeler that had been bullying me
since the Colorado Street Exit (that could kill us in the sedan), and
never seeing my offspring again.

Oh, those two blond, blue-eyed and beautiful, slick-as-cat's-ass
daughters, and that one brown-haired, brown-eyed and beautiful,
smart-as-shit daughter— gone forever! "If I should survive the crash.
Should I exit on the next ramp?" I wondered. No, I couldn't take the
chance for now eagle-eyed number one son could not even
distinguish that this mass of metal was automobiles, much less see
the blue hatchback, in the dark of the night. We drove on in blind
faith. I asked the Little Woman, "How far?" She replied that she
didn't know, for our freeway map would run out of freeway in about
seven miles where the San Diego, the Ventura, the San Berdoo, the
Santa Monica and the Golden State Freeways come to a fork.

Now I was truly terrified. I had no idea what to do. I couldn't even
get near an exit, much less exit on one. I had no idea where daughters
and the great white rabbit were. The detested pink gold in my tank
was rapidly dissipating. I saw nothing, but sharp-eyed son diverted
himself long enough to notice that the needle on the unleaded fuel
gauge was resting on E. He exclaimed, "Dad, we don't have any
gas!" I had enough gas in my belly at this point to travel to Boise,
Idaho and nature was calling.

I have inherited three things from my mother: her sparkling blue-
gray eyes; her anxiety attacks; and Meniere's Syndrome. All three
were working overtime, for both of us right now. I collected my
thoughts, ignoring the stomach cramps that were squeezing me like
a vise, and asked, "Do the girls know that old friend lives in
Ventura?" The Little Woman replied, not too reassuringly, that she
thought so.

Logic told me to stay on the Ventura Freeway. That should go to
Ventura, and I hoped for a break in the mass of metal. And there was

still no sight of daughters number one, two, and three and the great white rabbit. On I jerked—fifteen mph, thirty-five mph, twenty mph, fifty mph, zero mph and so on for the next hour. Finally eagle-eyed number one son spied the great white rabbit and the blue hatchback. "Thank you, Lord. Thank you, Allah. Oh, thank you, Buddha!" I had been praying to any Supreme Being that I thought would listen to me, and someone had heard. We quickly worked our way to the nearest exit to (a) fill up the tanks (b) empty my vise-like belly (c) find out where the hell old friend lived.

After accomplishing "a" and "b", I proceeded to "c." A typical, longhaired, blond, tanned, freckled; native Californian motor-head explained the maze of freeways to me. He got very tired of going over it ten times so my thick skull could absorb it. After twenty minutes I know he was wondering how this white-faced asshole could have found his way around the block, much less from the east.

Walking to the pay phone, which daughter number three has already occupied, I noticed him snickering with his native-born California lady. Paranoia again. Throwing my daughter from the booth, I called old friend who was wondering where we were, for she had made chicken for us. After being seven hours cooked, it was not too moist at this point. I explained where we were, and she guessed the optimum should be one hour, and diverted her plans accordingly.

It was nine thirty pm, PST, and I called Dr. Fred and explained briefly where we were. Dr. Fred's spouse had also prepared a sumptuous meal for us, and naturally it was of no use to anyone, save for a few starved coyotes. Dr. Fred told me they had lighted my way into California with the fire that was still raging in San Berdoo. He felt this was a good omen. I didn't. Oh, well, is the glass half-full of water or half-empty? It is all in the way you look at things. It must be easier looking at things when you are making $1000,000 plus per annum.

For some reason, I was looking for something in the blue hatchback, and in my rummaging I felt something was missing. The jack. "Where the hell is the jack?" Daughter number one replied, "What is a jack?" Daughter number two asked if I meant that bar with the grooves on it. I said, "Yes." She replied that when they were packing they felt that this was useless and didn't even know what it was. Since they weren't talking to me to find out what it was they had left it. "Left it where?", I asked. They looked at me as though I were a moron and said, "Back east, of course, Dad." What could have happened through three thousand miles of driving with no jack, I will leave to the reader's imagination.

We were again on our way with my freeway map to Old Friend's place-hand-drawn on a torn-up waxed McDonald's coke cup which said, "Put litter in its place." We went through the street that Old Friend lived on, but I couldn't make it out. Seventy-five uneventful minutes later we were at Old Friend's door. There is no finer feeling in the world than knowing that you will not sleep in a motel tonight. We dragged our racked bodies into Old Friend's kitchen. After much hugging and kissing, Old Friend called Son, daughter, daughter-in-law and son-in-law.

I had not seen either lad or lass for twenty years, since they had made the trek to California to seek their fortunes. From what I remembered Lass, number one, a female, was a wild young little gal. At her arrival, I noticed one thing had changed: she wasn't young anymore. Her husband, Lemmon, I think his name was, seemed about as personal and bright as a stick.

Enter Lad number two, a male. What I remembered about him was that he was a young, nice, freckled boy with sandy-brown hair. What I saw now was a drunken, sodden blot, extending a white, fish handshake. He was the spitting image of his deceased father, right down to the large mole that He had on his right cheek, under his eye, that made him always appeared as if he was looking over that at you. Lad number two's wife was a drunken, flirting "social bug," whose only intelligent mouthing was, "Fersher, I expected a Brooklyn accent." Brooklyn accent! I thought, "She doesn't even know where Pennsylvania is."

Next came Lad number two's offspring, two refugees from Hells Angels, I was sure, so I'd better watch my big mouth. They stayed just long enough to exchange un-pleasantries and insults and mount their cycles and leave, adding much to my happiness.

Lass number one's kids also arrived. One girl (I think) and one boy (I think). The female was equipped with everything that Lass number one was equipped with at her age, including a filthy tongue. Her mother looked on proudly as she rolled out four-letter words, like a sailor on leave. Lemmon's boy said nothing, but mentioned that they had invited Ronald Reagan to their wedding, but old Ronnie didn't show. I felt myself sinking into incredulity. How anyone could invite the Presidential candidate and actually believe that he would come, between his whistle-stopping and $1,000 per plate dinners, to attend Lemmon, Jr's wedding! I chuckled out loud and almost gave way to a fit of laughter.

I hadn't imbibed for ten years, and the Little Woman doesn't drink; mother doesn't drink; our daughter's don't drink; and, of course, number one son doesn't drink. Mother's non-drinking old friend shot a look over at my daughters. I could see her comparing them to her granddaughter. The comparison must not have set too well for she mentioned to Lemmon that his daughter should maybe curtail her in-port language. I wish I could be kinder about this reunion, but I call them as I see them.

My needs were many at this point. I owned six days worth of dirty clothes, and the jeans that I had on would probably have walked away if I had taken them off. I craved a shower and bed for my brood. I know I would never make it to Dr. Fred's that night, as it is fifty miles away and the time was now approaching one AM. Mother and old friend were reminiscing, and Lass and Lad number one and two were trying to reminisce, but I could not understand a word, because of their slurring from the booze. However, I looked as though I were paying attention. My favorite game, and they were too stoned to notice. I asked, in my smoothest tongue, praying for old friend's maternal instincts, for some food. I was so hungry by now I could have eaten sawdust. Now Old Friend watches pennies, to say the least, and she prepared the dried out chicken that had since dried away. It appeared, and she popped it into the microwave, that she proudly announced she had. I would have eaten this stuff raw at this point. I was not concerned with her one-up-manship of impressing mother with her microwave.

With my stomach full I felt now was the time to get the laundry done. Old Friend caught on quickly, and showed the Little Woman where she could find the washer and dryer. Sleeping arrangements had to be made; I am not going to sleep at Lass number one's house for sure. Mother was pre-arranged to sleep at Old Friend's, so Lad number two was the choice. I was hoping that the Hell's Angels roam the freeway till dawn and that we would have left for the Doc's house before they come home.

So the choice was settled on, and we headed for Lad number two's house, a very beautiful home. We stumbled in, and Lad number two wanted to chat. I didn't. He was unintelligible at this point, so I feigned sleep on the couch. He finally got the idea. He shook me awake, but I didn't move until the third shake— just to make sure he believed I was asleep. He showed us to our room, his own bedroom. I flopped on the bed with the Little Woman after five nights in motels, and three nights of sleeping in a crowd. We are at last alone. I was about to exercise my male instincts, but it was to no avail. The Little Woman was fast asleep, mouth open and snoring…a not-so-good situation. The count: no balls and one strike. I fell into a deep sleep.

We awoke at nine am, one week before Thanksgiving, 1980. I stumbled to the table for my salvation and inspiration—coffee—to find the Little Woman awake and chatting with Lad number two. He was sucking on a Coors, and "social bug" was not being social at all, having all the earmarks of a monumental hangover. Having had that feeling many times myself, I could almost empathize with her. But I immediately dismissed the thought and drank the warm, brown come-aliver, coffee. I then noticed "social bug" flitting to the frig for her second eye-opener, and Lad number two barked, "Me, too." After three cans apiece, they were rolling again, kitchy cooing and lovey doving, when number one Lass burst in with her payroll checking account book.

It seems Lemmon and she had started a business and were doing very well, so Old Friend said. Lass number one was relating to me, eyeing me through two hellacious red peepers, that I certainly was glad I was not looking through on this fine sunny Southern California morning, that she just must make the payroll today. I saw her balance and wouldn't have wanted to be one of her fifteen employees, for the amount she was paying out to those peons did not coincide with what her account stated. She missed it by about $1,600. Oh, well, nice game of one-up-manship by this master.

I dragged myself to shower among some posies on the wall, and I thought, "Our peacocks aren't so bad after all." I was dressed and the Little Woman was dressed and packed. Lass one and Lad two were weaving, slurring, and bobbing, and it was only eleven am. The "social bug" was really getting social. I gave our thanks, and we prepared to leave, when Lad and Lass numbers one and two began discussing who was going to have the Thanksgiving and Christmas Day festivities, for which we were invited. It was decided that Thanksgiving would be with Lad number two, and Christmas Eve at Lass number ones.

We departed for Dr. Fred's . The little blue hatchback was planted in the mirror again and dutifully following the bronze sedan, east to Los Angeles, Glendale, and Pasadena.

A busload of convicts from Chino prison, in a big white caged bus, had all spotted daughters number one, two, and three at the same time they were making every obscene gesture imaginable at my offspring. It was afternoon, and the traffic was heavy, but not as bad as last night, so I was able to maneuver us away from the band of cutthroats. This was much to the Little Woman's relief, for they were starting to zero in on her too.

We went down the Orange Freeway, south to the Pomona Freeway to where Dr. Fred resided.

We were greeted by Dr. Fred's spouse, number one son, Manuel, and number two son, Martin, and spouse's mother, smiling with gold teeth abounding. We entered and, at once, the Little Woman and Dr. Fred's wife were reminiscing. I was on the couch with Manuel and Martin climbing, jabbing, poking, slobbering on, and slapping me.

Dr. Fred's wife had really increased her disciplining. I saw Martin open a fifty-pound bag of rice, which he threw at anyone or anything he saw, but mostly at Manuel. He then jumped from the kitchen bar onto Martin's leg, and of course screaming ensured. Daughters number one, two, and three already have had enough of this and announced they were going for a ride. I screamed "You have no jack," but they said, "It doesn't matter," and left. I eagerly awaited Dr. Fred's return, for I needed him desperately for confirmation of the house and my employment.

He returned at seven, saying that he would be on call all night, and we should select our rooms. What a mansion! Dr. Fred was doing OK— rooms all over. He had a BMW, Mercedes, nice tailor-made suits, and a monstrous diamond ring. The fellow is getting richer by the month is seemed. In the six weeks it took me to return, he had acquired even more, but it looked as though Dr. Fred's wife was going bald.

Dr. Fred remarked on how well everyone looked, and this made me feel good, for Dr. Fred is a very knowledgeable physician. We talked for hours while Martin and Manuel were literally destroying the mansion. It was starting to show earmarks of those two darlings. Crayons, red, blue, and green, in large xs and os adorned the beautiful large living room walls. There was a spot on the rug, which still announced a missed trip to the toilet. All in all, though, it was a pleasurable four hours. He announced that he would make a phone call to get the key to our rent-free house. To show everyone with pride, his and mine, the house that he and I had picked out six weeks ago. We followed Dr. Fred to the mansion of the doctor who owned the home, a Dr. Renaldo Arriga, who was so graciously letting me live in this home rent-free. "What a wonderful little surgeon." I kept telling the Little Woman; but she was saying very little on our way to the Arriga home. Dr. Renaldo wasn't in, but lovely, smiling Mrs. Arriga was, and she handed over the key and wished us success and happiness. On to the new home in San Dimas! I was happy again, exclaiming over and over, "This is great!"

We followed Dr. Fred's silver Mercedes through winding roads and freeways, finally hooking up with the right one, and soared up the hill, up and up, to our mansion in the sky.

The Mansion in the Sky

(Someone Else Lives Here, Too)

It was eight pm when we arrived on the driveway and of course the electricity was not on. So Dr. Fred and I were armed with flashlights for the showing to the Little Woman, daughters one, two and three and number one son. The key opened the door, and the view was breathtaking. With the star lit sky, the lake glistening and the large palms swaying in the cool evening breeze, Dr. Fred and I were running around inside trying to show the house, the redwood and carpeting, all the rooms, patio, grapefruit trees and lemon trees. But the Little Woman wasn't saying anything. Daughter number three spoke, "Not bad". Those were the first words she had uttered in my direction since Kansas City, which seemed like light years ago. Somehow the house didn't seem as kind to me as it had at our first meeting. Number one son decided that he was afraid of the dark door, and we felt it best to wait for daylight to really see it.

When we were departing, as I was backing down our driveway, I hit something—a ledge jutting out of the house. Under the light of the very bright moon I saw a gash in my new, only four-thousand-miles-on-it, steel belted radial. The cost to replace was fifty – six dollars at Archers Texaco Station in San Deamon. The Little Woman muttered to Dr. Fred that she would give the house the benefit of the doubt till morning light. I knew then that the battle was lost. I had lost valuable ground in my quest for the land of golden opportunity. However, I did have the key in pocket to our rent-free mansion in the sky.

Now all there was to do was call phone, electric, water, and gas companies to make it habitable. This would be done first thing in the morning so on I went to sweet dreams, of life in the golden state.

I was thinking of getting in some martial action with the Little Woman for I had cleverly selected the room farthest away from everyone else. However it was to no avail, for number one son was afraid in his strange, new environment. The count: no balls and strike two.

We awoke at six am to really get moving on settling into our mansion in the sky. We had previously shipped, via UPS, twenty boxes of necessities to Dr. Fred's home, and these must be driven to our new abode. I was nervously anticipating my Little Woman's reaction to her new home; for, as you may recall, she had mumbled that she would wait till dawn's early light to judge. Dr. Fred told us as we walked out the door to load boxes and ourselves into the bronze sedan, that we would awaken in our bedroom to the view of the lake in the morning. "How glorious!" I thought. My thoughts of glory were interrupted by my remembering that she hadn't yet seen the peacocks on the bedroom walls.

Off we drove with instructions, again handwritten on paper, to get to our new home. "Do we turn here?" "No…next," and so on. It took one hour for what should have been a fifteen-minute drive. It felt with my poor sense of direction, I would have some trouble with this entanglement of concrete and paint, but right then there were other problems to solve.

I noticed the mailbox was broken and looked weather-beaten. Something else that wasn't there before was now in the corral of the very impressive house next door. It was the biggest, blackest, bull I had ever seen. He was coming down the incline and smashed into the fence bordering our property. "Good God," I muttered. Everyone was running away at a very good clip, up the driveway to our newly acquired home. I noticed the ledge had a black scuffmark on it, the spot where my radial had died.

Into the house we went. I was pointing out the exotic palms and the many different cactus, when a lizard ran across daughter number two's foot. This broke the mood that I was trying to set as her shrieking set off a veritable chorus. Everyone finally settled into low hysteria, and we resumed the tour. Number one son was ecstatic with the pond and had visions of sharks swimming in there.

The Little Woman had seen enough, however, and screamed, "This is disgusting!" There is no kitchen, no work area, the place stinks, there are no closets, and those strolling peacocks are ridiculous. I hate it! I hate it!" "Well, fellow," I told myself, "you'd better dip into your selling bag of tricks FAST." I drew a blank. She left the house via the patio door. Unfortunately, at that moment, a lizard was caught between doors, and it scurried in again. Only this time, it ran across the Little Woman's foot. She stood sobbing on the patio wall overlooking the lake, the mountains and the airport. I was looking into the living room mirror, not looking at all like Steve McQueen, but sort of like Lee Harvey Oswald in his Dallas mug shot. She was sobbing, "There is no dishwasher. You told me the carpeting was rust. The kitchen floor is a mess. There is a mouse nest under the dryer in the unheated garage." I kept saying, "But just look at the view." She just sobbed.

Daughters number one, two, and three were wandering cautiously. I counted lizards by the number of shrieks. Number one son was sitting in his dry pond, making like a frogman, and he wanted water in it.

I had made all the necessary calls that morning, and all was well, save for the electricity. The electric man couldn't get to us for two weeks.

The Little Woman was settling down now to mild hysteria. I pulled myself together. "Well let's get those boxes unpacked." We unpacked clothes, clothes, and more clothes, dishes, pots, pans, knick-knacks, and spices. HER SPICES?...

Finally, trip after trip, everything was unpacked, but not put in its place, for the Little Woman had realized her dilemma and started to clean. Now, when the Little Woman cleans, she cleans. We had borrowed Dr. Fred's vacuum, but it could not be used as electricity had not arrived.

The Little Woman was a blur of activity. The water was on, because they were building a house below us, and they were using our water and they were paying for it. This brightened her spirits a tad. She was a whirlwind; dusting everything; pulling out drawers and dousing them with water outside.

Number one son discovered the water was on and figured I had lied to him. He took the hose and started filling his pond.

Daughter number one had announced that she had just found a diamond earring in the rug and was very happy—this lady could spot a diamond on Pike's Peak from Topeka on a snowy day. I felt this was an omen. (I was starting to believe in them, but couldn't distinguish the good from the bad.)

Now a very strange incident occurred—one of many to come. The Little Woman had lined up every drawer from kitchen cabinets (all orange) on the patio to dry, after scrubbing and scouring them. The warm sun had dried them, so she took the hose and doused them for good measure, and cleaned them again. The sun was setting and doubling the sunset in the calm lake. I was somewhat serene, and we walked to the patio to collect the eight drawers, for it would be getting dark soon, and we had no electricity. There it was, right before my eyes— matching diamond earrings, exactly the mate of my daughter's find. Naturally, at this time we assumed daughter number one had left the earring, thinking it might hatch in the warm sun. I was sure that would be the only reason she would leave that diamond there. We called her from her bedroom, and she produced the original from her purse. How could this be? There was no way, after the Little Woman had cleaned, that anything could have survived. Yet, here the mate was sitting on drawer number three, basking in the evening sun. No one had the slightest idea how it got there. I didn't know about anyone else, but a cold chill ran up my back, in that warm California sunset.

Since the electricity controls the heat, back we went to Dr. Fred's for the evening. I stopped at a pay phone. Daughter number three had beaten me to it, and I had to remove her again. I called Dr. Fred and told him that he would have live-ins for two weeks. He was most accommodating and assured me, "No problem; my mansion is your mansion."

Off we went to find a Pizza Hut for one thick and chewy and one thin and crispy pizza.

After dinner, we drove back to Dr. Fred's with the little blue hatchback in my rearview mirror again. I was getting better; the trip took only fifty minutes. "I have knocked ten minutes off the trip the very first day," I thought smugly.

I thought back to our find, the earring, and I felt we were definitely not alone, but I said nothing to anyone at Dr. Fred's. I sat in Dr. Fred's living room without Dr. Fred, for he was on a mission of mercy, saving precious life and collecting his fee, of course. Manuel and Martin were busy destroying the dishwasher—Martin using Manuel's chunky little body for a battering ram. Dr. Fred's spouse didn't mind, but mother seemed to and whacked Martin with a pot right on his little ass. Manuel was crying, Martin also, and momma was screaming in a foreign tongue. It was probably better that I didn't know what she was saying because she was really yelling now.

She then cut off the harangue and gestured to me with her hand to her mouth, meaning, "Do you want to eat?" I shook my head negatively and tried to explain by hand movements that we had consumed a thick and chewy and thin and crispy, but to no avail.

I just walked upstairs to my newly found love nest, and darned if I didn't fall asleep before the Little Woman even arrived. The score: no balls and three strikes, and I'm out.

Dawn broke early at 23406 Sandy Hill Road, and off we drove to our home that we can't live in because of the electric man. We were to meet "gas man" who said he would meet us at eight thirty am sharp, and we were not to be late. I didn't even know this man and already I disliked him. He arrived one half hour late—"Couldn't find the damn place." He began lighting pilots here and there. I must say he will never be a public relations man for Southern California Gas

Company. Everything was a chore, and he swore aloud after every little task was completed. I was getting angry with this homely little fat man with his golden tan. I said nothing until he almost stomped over my little number one son. I growled, "Hey fellow, watch where you're going." He said nothing, but went about his appointed rounds. He then said, "That will be forty-five dollars for turning all this stuff on, refundable one year from today and no interest paid." I grumbled on, and got two twenties and a five dollar bill from the Little Woman. He scribbled a receipt and went for the door. Before leaving, he gave me the piece de resistance "You have a damn gas leak to the hot water heater." He went to his truck. I ran out the door wanting to question this man further, for I had visions of us all being blown to bits some lovely California evening. I asked "What?" He replied, "I wouldn't worry about it, though, because you probably won't be here that long." Off he sped in a cloud of dust, down the winding hill and out of sight.

Ferdinand, the Bull, was now watching me intently. The Little Woman again was grousing about the house but continued to clean. I feel she releases her frustrations this way. I knew to stay out of her way and went to trim all of our lovely plants and newly seen cactus, palms, lemon and grapefruit trees.

The day passed quickly, for I was thrilled with every new item and treasure I found, except for the cast-off snakeskins.

The shrieks seemed to be stabilizing at seven, so there were seven lizards living with us. I noticed that a monster hawk was perched atop a very skinny dried-out palm, and he was watching me, pardon the pun—"like a hawk." Who knows, a possible pear tree with a partridge might appear. I can't wait for the nine ladies dancing, but not looking forward to ten Lords a leaping. There was not a cloud in the sky, and I noticed that I was turning pink from the warm California sun. I would be golden brown soon, and it was three days before Thanksgiving. I was starting to get the cobwebs out, and was thinking again, as I continued to cut, trim and weed.

We awoke on Thanksgiving Day to find Martin and Manuel doing what they had been doing for the last week systematically making the beautiful new home into a not so beautiful old home.

They were decorating with crayons and tearing out the landscaping in chunks of various flowers and Japanese lanterns, and finding many snails. The shrieks were starting again with daughters number one, two and three, as the two masters of mayhem were putting the snails in various places around the house. Dr. Fred's mother-in-law solved this problem by cooking them—the snails, not the kids— unfortunately. The houseboy had disappeared and I asked no questions. Dr. Fred finally confided that the yellow bruise under Martin's right eye was put there by his twenty-year old houseboy. Dr. Fred, rather than instituting a child-abuse charge against him, purchased a one-way ride to the Orient and bade him a fond farewell. I could almost share old houseboy's feeling for these little darlings, for they were trying my patience, and I was getting weaker by the moment.

It was Thanksgiving Evening, and we were ready to go to Lad number two's house for the festivities, when the phone rang. Burly Curly, it seemed, was freezing his ass off in some shopping center phone booth in the great northeast. His mother and father had cut off his phone privileges, and he had to seek outside help to reach out and touch daughter number one across North America to convey his love.

At last we were all packed into the bronze sedan and off to Lad number two's house for Thanksgiving dinner. We arrived after a one-hour drive, and I noticed something I hadn't noticed before, a brown, dung-like color all around me and in the distance. Before I had always laughed at the Bob Hope-isms and Johnnie's clever pokes at the California smog. However, now it was not so humorous as daughters number one and two and three were gasping and the Little Woman's eyes were tearing and smarting. The brown haze was so thick around, us that although we were in Los Angeles, I could just barely make out the skyline of the few tall buildings LA possesses.

With the smog and my poor sense of direction, I could not find Lad number two's house. But wisely I did have his phone number. I called him. He remarked slurringly that I was only three blocks from his home, and uttered something which I made out to be "stupid son-of-a-bitch." He condescended to come and meet us. He arrived screeching to a halt and skidding in his 1956 done-over Ford pickup that he felt I should just be overwhelmed with.

Now my love for anything mechanical is just this: if it will get me from point A to point B, I won't even touch a hood latch, much less probe into that dirty mess, the engine. In my teenage years when all my peers were greasy and oily from morn till eve, I always stayed sparkling clean and odor free by being very clumsy at even distinguishing a crescent wrench from a pair of pliers. They became so disgusted with this idiot that they would finally fix my car by themselves, and think that I was the most inept fifteen fingered human being alive. (This trick still works well to this day.) So, you can understand that the 1956, pickup under-whelmed me a bunch.

Entering Lad number two's house, I found the Hell's Angels sitting on the floor studying daughters number one and two and three and undressing them with their watery, glazed eyes. Lemmon and Lemmon Jr. were playing ping-pong. Old Friend and mother were talking on the couch. Lass number one was moaning about the virus that she had picked up somewhere. I knew where! The Kit Kat Club in a brown bottle! But with her wrap-around California shades on to hide the eyes, everyone believed this tale. I, for one would still not care to be looking through those eyes, cool California or not. They all chided me for having on a light brown suit. They looked like unmade beds, with their Honda and Kawasaki tee shirts on. They said, "I must conform to the easy California life now that I was a native". They even attempted to stain my suit with coffee by making false trips on the rug. They succeeded.

I couldn't find Lass number one's daughter about, but I found out later that she had grabbed a six-pack of Coors and retired to one of the bedrooms with her latest beau. I didn't see him or her for the duration, but did hear enough grunts and groans to assure me that she was in good hands.

Social Butterfly was feeling no pain, and introduced the Little Woman and me to her mother. She was a pretty, late Sixtyish grandmother who, from her finery, I felt must have done all right for herself.

Lemmon coaxed me into a game of ping-pong for this was the

extent of his athletic ability. I tried not to notice how uncoordinated he was, even though Old Friend and Lass number one had praised his prowess as the best ping-pong player in Southern California. I beat him twenty-four to four. He was pissed off, and since I wanted to eat that free dinner I pretended that I had been very lucky and suddenly became very clumsy with the paddle. The moron was still beaten by eleven points. I passed it off as my lucky day and with a straight face, assured him that he was certainly a champ.

Now Lemmon Jr. wanted me at the green table, and from observing him I knew that I probably could beat him left handed and blindfolded while eating that dinner which I hadn't had yet. I took no chances of beating a lad of such obvious talents, but I noticed Old Friend looking as though she was catching on to my act.

We finally did eat and enjoy the free dinner. I tried to run, but no such luck, for Lad number two's aging Flower Children friends arrived. They were both stoned and were holding forth on capitalism and the establishment. I was ready to jump in, for they couldn't take that meal away now, but the Little Woman saw what I was about to do and led me out to look at the brown California sunset.

Four hours of nonsense had passed, and I noticed Social Butterfly's mother was not vertical now but horizontal, with her very well groomed head resting on the first step of the stairs, that lead to Lad number two's love-nest. She was smashed, loaded, pickled, and mumbling that everyone had mistaken her for Gloria Swanson at a party last week. They collected her very smoothly as though they had done it many times before, and propped her up in a chair where she remained, and might possibly still be for all I know.

Her two darling Hell's Angels grandchildren were seriously contemplating taking her a motorcycle ride on the Ventura Freeway to Oxnard, to show her off to the group, I assumed.

Daughter number three received (I don't know how) a phone call from super Jock. The expressions of all the lovely people there spelled out their opinions of her as a tramp and trollop. Mother, being overly sensitive, felt she must defend her granddaughter to these pillars of society by saying "isn't love grand?"

They started to discuss Christmas Eve with Lass number one, and I thought, "Absolutely not for me!" I wouldn't care if they had the cash receipts from Disneyland for the month of December that I could rummage through freely, for the whole evening. I was not going through this again. I regretted that I would be extremely busy and couldn't possibly make it, with the house and all, work, adjusting, and my sanity. Thank you, but no thanks. Old Friend I felt sure was on to me now but I will never know. In the next eighteen and one half months of our life in California I would not see any of this group again except when I picked mother up on December twenty-third for her flight back east with daughters one, two, and three.

We departed for Dr. Fred's house in a warm, smoggy, bronze sedan on a warm, smoggy California Freeway to the tune that has been haunting me since Pop's Oasis, Blondie's "The Tide is High."

On the day after Thanksgiving, as I was watching football on Dr. Fred's TV there came a question from Dr. Fred's spouse, "How do they play baseball?" I ignored this until little Martin began to parrot dear mom by asking me over and over "What is this? What is this? How does that work? What are the men doing on the baseball field?"

I finally gave up and drove to the McDonald's off the fifty-seven freeway for a cup of serenity. And waited for my meeting with the little smiling man who had assured me eight weeks ago not to worry about "nothing." After meeting him that evening, I found, that I did indeed have much to worry about. He barely recognized me, much less being ready to give me an important position in his firm. His excuse was that he hadn't really believed I was coming back, that things had changed, and some more nonsense to which I was now paying no attention at all. I was quietly sobbing, hoping Dr. Fred would not notice, for he was highly embarrassed by all this nonsense.

After I settled down, I figured "ok well, one out of two isn't bad" for I still had the key to our rent-free, mortgage free home in my pocket, and I was clutching it for dear life.

The Adjustment

"Electric Man" day finally arrived. Unlike the gas man, he was a very cordial and amiable fellow who didn't even ask for a deposit for he said that Southern California Edison would bill us the first month for our deposit, for they understood how it was to make a move such as this. "No problem." I liked him very much.

We moved into our dream house on this, the eighth day of December 1980, and I retired to the patio for the temperature was approaching ninety-five degrees at ten AM this December morning now to thoroughly tan my now pink body and face. Oh, glorious sun! I found out in the evening that John Lennon had been shot.

I tried to figure out what I was going to do about sustaining life and limb in the land of golden opportunity. The little smiling man who said, "Not to worry about nothing," was not even returning my frantic phone calls on our new green (to go with the peacocks) touch-tone phones that don't work worth a pinch of sour owlshit. This was a constant thorn in my side until we found Ma Bell eight months later. The phone company to which I allude well be very familiar to all California readers who already know the name of this infamous line of communications in the land of plenty. This phone company was famous for cutting off your conversation in the first thirty seconds, or perhaps waiting for ten minutes; that was part of the surprise. The phones were also out of order five times in our first seven days. I found myself calling the repair service from my phone booth in the gas station on Arrow Highway, only to be cut off in my

53

pleading with Operator seventeen, to whom I always seemed to talk, and with whom I became very friendly. This was a never-ending battle with the phones, and one I never conquered. Phones were never fixed, but the company always sent you disconnect notices one day before the current month's bill came. Daughter's number one and three had their only link to the outside world of Burly Curly and Super Jock disrupted many times, and I now had a mutiny on my hands. It did hinder any readjustment that they even remotely may have considered.

Every day I scoured the LA Times for employment opportunities among the many classified ads for jobs, and wandered to many employment agencies to no avail. Amid the pile of resumes that were being sent and phone calls being made to prospective employers, I was much aware that the glowing tan that I now possessed was not pouring dollars into our now shrinking bank account. I was praying on a regular bases every chance I could for anything that would bring money into our lives. De' Fred's cliché, "We will not let you starve," was not heard again.

Finally, on December twelfth, our first Christmas card arrived from the East and that had everyone near tears. In this glowing golden land of opportunity one tends to forget about "tis the season to be jolly," and I never quite got used to the bikini and scantily-clad ladies, and sweat pouring from my head and down my back and into the crack in my ass, during Christmas season. We had now settled into what I would call this Yule Tide Season of ninety degree heat, Christmas 1980: a very homesick, unsettled, anxious and sometimes frightful time.

Oh well, on to Christmas shopping. Out into the extreme heat we went to Southern California's finest stored buying everything on plastic. We shopped all day and into the night, and then returned home to find our house lit up like a Christmas tree, outside lights and inside lights on. Everyone was scared to death of going in. As we were driving up our driveway, the inside lights went off, sending shrieks and moans through daughters number one, two, and three and the Little Woman. There was nothing to do now but be brave. I was selected to enter the house alone and unarmed except for a pocketful of rocks that I had picked up. Slamming open the door against the wall, as I'd seen John Wayne do many times on the late show, I entered. Going through the house! I was as scared as one human being could ever be, and still be alive. –Nothing-. I was now getting my manhood back, and my mouth was resuming normal saliva flow. My hand was clutching the rock so tightly it hurt, and still—nothing! Thank God! I was satisfied and went to tell my females that all was well, but obviously they had driven to points unknown until I had corralled these intruders.

I stood outside on the patio overlooking the beautiful night drama of shimmering water, small aircraft landing in between the lights that designated where they should go, and hearing the sounds that only a desert can produce. I felt very strongly that I was not alone, and considered heading East for the first time since the euphoria of the golden land had caught my fancy.

Everyone returned reluctantly, and even more reluctantly entered our furniture-less home—empty save for a portable fifteen-inch Sony, that Dr. Fred had bought for us out of sheer desperation. Come tomorrow I would make the furniture arrangements, and I instructed the Little Woman to make a list of necessities to have shipped. I meant the bare necessities for money was getting to be a premium item. Before saying goodnight, I heard daughter's number one, two and three keeping me to my word of flying them back East for the twenty-forth of December. It was ten days away.

They were running up the tab on the phone bill, calling every domestic airline, setting their itineraries and mother's. After this, I scolded that I would take care of it. Their looks told me of their disbelief. Mother was also getting rammy at Old friends. It seems things with Lass and Lad were getting unreal, with all of the groups not so amusing antics. Daughter number one was using this as a great wedge, knowing I had control over them, but not mother. I assured them that it would be taken care of by the end of the week, and it was. Thank you, Crossroads Travel, Chris, and American Express, to the tune of $880.00 for a twelve-month payment plan on a Capital Super Saver direct LAX to JFK on December twenty-seventh, 1980.

Departure eight-forty-five a.m.—five-forty-five p.m. arrival to the waiting arms of Super Jock and Burly Curly, who arrived at JFK at ten in the morning to be certain not to miss our little darlings. Things were going from bad to worse.

"Call me Tom," said that this small shipment of furniture would be four weeks in coming; the girls hate the school, the kids and the entire California educational system. After three trips to the Saints of San Deamons High School, with the milquetoast staff, I found I had to agree with them.

Much to my dismay, the Little Woman was now complaining about how she hated this house, and that now she had found three good new pairs of pantyhose missing. The howls of coyotes in the dark always sent a very cold feeling from my feet to the top of my head. The curtains were moving, when there was no breeze and not moving when there was a breeze. The Little Woman also announced that if I wanted clean clothes I'd better go in that garage and kill the green lizard that was keeping her company while she did the laundry. Number one son was crying, for he had just crushed one of the three dozen varieties of fish that he had purchased to fill his pond, on the patio, in our rent-free home He had turned over a very large rock on the little fellow.

Phone call after phone call came from Super Jock and Burly Curly, one almost every four hours in our waking moments. I was to find out later that Burly Curly had the larger phone bill of the two during our stay in California. In one month he spent $210, while Super Jock followed with a mere $146.

I felt beaten and discouraged, but I pressed on. The way things were, I really had no idea why I was still holding onto my dream. But after all, I did accomplish my golden tan, which for me was an excellent reason for pushing on.

The day slid and oozed by, bringing more Christmas cards and some packages for the kids, who would not even look at me at this point. They were clutching their very own airline tickets in hand, never leaving those little pieces of letters and numbers, punched out by the computer, out of their sight. The Little Woman awakened one morning with an eye that looked like she had gone ten rounds with Jack Dempsey and accused me of hitting her in her sleep.

I knew what that feeling of not being alone was now—the new pantyhose that had disappeared earlier had returned. We were living in a haunted house! I dared not mention this to anyone as my diamond-earring-daughter was also suspicious, for she confided in me that her makeup kit had disappeared also.

I now sat on our carpeted floor looking into our mirrored walls after a full day's bout with filling the waterbed. I typed a Christmas greeting to my sister, Alice, in the cold, snowy Great Northeast to the tune on the radio of Blondie's "The Tide is High."

December 21, 1980
San Dimas, CA
Christmas, 1980

Dear Alice,
Greetings from a very different environment. Now that things are settling enough for a realistic evaluation, I can say that I like it very well. The two girls and the Little Woman have made it a little tough, but I understand they really don't want to be here. Daughter number one isn't too bad, but she does have her moments. Number one son has never been happier, excited from the time he wakes up until he goes to bed. I can't believe it. It's going to take time for all of us.

The doc has been great. Our furniture hasn't arrived yet, so he insisted on buying us a small TV. Feels good to know there are good people left here, too. The furniture should arrive January twenty-forth, 1981. The prime rate went up again, woe is me. I check on mother frequently. She is being treated with nothing but kindness since she arrived at Old Friend's. I'm impressed (I fibbed), I can understand that also. (Seems like I'm understanding quite a bit lately.) Hmm!

By the time this letter reaches you, you will be a flying veteran. Give my best to your son Ricky. I'm sure your Christmas will be good, being with him. How is work? I really feel you are going to climb the corporate ladder there, no kidding. Things sure have changed. Wow!

Daughter number one just came back from giving mother her ticket. She was glad to get it. They are leaving December twenty-seventh, from LAX at eight-forty-five a.m., arriving JFK five-forty-five p.m. What a father doesn't do for his daughters! I hope they come back. They are looking forward to seeing you. I'm glad they do respect and admire you. Give them a little pitch that their father is not trying to hurt them, the opportunity for them is tremendous. Hopefully, they will understand this someday. Daughter number one is going to Las Vegas tomorrow with Dr. Fred and spouse, reluctantly. I can't figure it out—the other two also had the chance, but they declined.

We've had some ups and downs too numerous to mention, but I will tell you the waterbed story. This gigantic waterbed was left here by the previous owner, so I proceeded to fill it with a hose that was too short and leaked. This was ten or eleven in the morning, get the picture? The hose leaked right at the coupling on the nozzle, which, as you know, was too short. Four and a half hours later, it was filled. I'm excited and proud. Number one son is excited. Daughter number one is excited. The Little Woman is almost excited, and the other two girls could care less. Now, remember, the hose had been leaking all this time into the frame of the bed. We bailed. I was still excited and proud, and number one son was excited; and daughter number one was excited. The Little Woman, you can imagine after a washload of towels soaked from the bailing and sopping up water as well—I'll leave that to your imagination. The girls could care less. Finally, the bed was full, towels were dry, and we loved it. The girls could care less. Number one son was jumping around, I was wallowing in the bed; daughter number one was happy; even the Little Woman, by this time, was getting excited. The girls could still care less. Then it happened. Number one son found the leak—a nice round pinhole in the bed on the right upper corner. The bed was full of water, which weighs about a ton, and the mattress was immovable. The Little Woman ran out to get a tire-patching kit which would not work because we could not keep the hole dry long enough to patch it. Finally, daughter number one came to the rescue with some glue that dries faster than it comes out of the tube. After one hour, success. We had to drain one-tenth of the water, and it was now nine-forty-five p.m. I was excited; number one son was excited; daughter number one was proud; the Little Woman was screaming; and the girls could care less. Now to sleep in this monster. Aaah great!

I will close for now. Give my love to all.

Fondly,
Your Brother
P.S. Merry Christmas and Happy New Year.

Did you notice how I wanted so badly to tell her what really was going on but skirted the real issue? The real story was not about the waterbed, which was true. I was trying in my very own way to tell her that I knew I had made the largest mistake of my mistake-filled thirty-seven years. "Greetings from a different environment." How true! From sanity to an insane asylum. "Now that things are settling for a realistic evaluation", meant now, that I have realized the mistake. When she reads this book she will know that "the letter," was a desperate cry for help, a three thousand mile plea that I didn't have enough brains to make. Alice and son, Ricky, thought the letter very amusing, so I did cover it well. So, on to the lie about mother being happy at Old Friends selfish, drunken, inconsiderate, loveless offspring's home. Mother would have flown a bi-plane across North America with a scarf blowing in the wind, even if it took two days, to get out of there. "We've had some ups and downs, too numerous to mention." What a crock of shit! Ups and downs! More like plummeting into "Dante's Inferno."

We traveled to Ventura to pick up mother, for her trip back east, and to introduce her to our domain. On the way back, she mentioned that Lemmon's great love is Miss Piggy because no matter what he's doing, when it's time for the Muppets, he drops everything even Lass number one, I assume, and devotes his undivided attention to the tube on which she appears. The lovely Miss Piggy, now that I think about it, she isn't bad compared to Lass number one. Lemmon Sr. is not all that dumb, and my opinion of him has changed.

With the furniture not having arrived, and mother staying with us until the twenty-seventh, she had two choices on where to sleep: our waterbed, whose leak had mysteriously stopped; or the floor. She chose the floor. Imagine putting your seventy-six-year old mother on the floor. The guilt overwhelms me. But mother is also very lovingly tough, and she endures.

We decided that for a Christmas present we would take mother to Disneyland, and Christmas Eve dawned to a very unlikely ninety-seven degrees. I did my sunbathing on the patio, and I gave strict orders that my mother was to be told nothing of the shed snakeskin that I had found there. She is deathly afraid of even a picture of a snake, much less the real thing. The Little Woman informed me, that she will tell her, if I don't take her back east immediately. I almost weakened, but she relented.

There was no furniture, a dried out Christmas tree, a few packages scattered here and there and the Christmas cards taped to the mirror, were already starting to cover the floor, and no one was even picking them up. A small TV blared white, in the one-lamp room, and the thermometer showed ninety degrees. I compared it to one short year ago—a houseful of furniture, a large full Christmas tree decorated to the teeth, an abundance of presents around the tree. There was a very good nip in the air and Christmas carols from the Mormon Tabernacle Choir solemnly playing, from our now-in-storage stereo. I almost wept at what I had done to the people I love most in the world, and retired to the patio to say a prayer.

Disneyland on Christmas we enjoyed, but mother didn't. She confided to me, at the end of the day, that her cataracts were so bad that she didn't see a thing. I flinched—another good deed gone to pot.

Home we went with the little blue hatchback in my mirror again; and, of course, instead of taking the Orange Freeway north, I became confused and headed for the city of Orange on the Five Freeway. We were close to Los Angeles before I could backtrack to the Pomona Freeway and home.

The next few days passed uneventfully, and December twenty-seventh arrived for the long-awaited flight back to Super Jock and Burly Curly and friends. I have seen daughters number one, two and three happy before, but I have never seen them happier than this. They were jubilant and had the car packed before I even arose. We arrived at LAX at seven-ten a.m. and they were ready to pass through the x-ray machine without even saying goodbye, or go take a hike, or anything. They were so happy to be getting the hell out of here I had to cajole them for a little hug. They obliged with a very little hug. Mother's fear of flying returned, and she looked at me as though she would never see me again. Off they flew to the waiting arms of Super Jock and Burly Curly who were already at JFK for one hour and forty-five minutes anxiously awaiting my loving daughters. I hoped silently that they would have their virginity intact when they returned—whenever that might be.

The drive back home could be compared to being in the last car at a funeral. I said nothing; the Little Woman said nothing; and number one son was worrying if the sun had boiled his fish. The house was empty as it had been except for daughter number one's makeup kit, which had now returned. Now the Little Woman's bra and slip were among the missing. I noticed my collar clip was gone from the pocket of my suit where I had left it yesterday.

On this sunny afternoon the doorbell rang, and a smartly dressed gentleman was standing there smiling in his shorts, knee-high socks and a madras shirt. He introduced himself as the neighborhood Welcomer and asked to come in. "Of course," I invited him in. The Little Woman was depleting our cash by going food shopping. He entered, and I apologized for having no furniture, but he understood and stood. Along with being a Welcomer, he also was collecting for a hospital in the area. I wrote a check for a massive five dollars. He grimaced, but did take the check and slipped it into his pocket. He then asked where we were from. "Pennsylvania."

"How long had we been here?" "Five weeks." I answered. "Do we like it?" "Yes and no."

"It takes time," he said. He told me that he has lived here for twenty-eight years, and also told me how to keep the rattlesnakes out. He was sure we had them, and we needed to watch our step. You place aluminum foil around the patio and this will keep them out. It does, save for one hearty rattler who had ignored the foil to sun himself on the patio one fine Sunday morning.

He also talked about the airport, and he remembered, as a pilot twenty-five years ago, that he used to fly over this spot when this house was nothing but a piece of the mountain.

He also went into detail about a murder that had taken place in the "sparking spot" that was at the bottom of our driveway twenty-three or twenty-four years ago. It seems that a young girl had been murdered one fine warm evening by her lover, and the case had never been solved. It had been the talk of the area that a fine young girl of sixteen could be killed as easy as that. A manhunt ensued with cops all over the place, he said, climbing up and down this mountain like flies. He just couldn't understand how this murder could not be solved, after all these years. I asked if this house was here at that time, and he said yes. I felt a chill about the few events he had described. I wondered again about the ever-present stench that the Little Woman couldn't even ammonia or Lysol out. Welcomer left, wishing number one son and me a good day and good luck and disappearing down hill. Walking briskly, I noticed Ferdinand the bull, eyeing me as though he would charge and stomp me to death if I made one more move toward that fence. I beat a slow but even retreat back to the house.

I awakened for the tenth time or so to the sound of our garbage cans and garbage being strewn about by our nocturnal friends, the coyotes. "Those bastards," I muttered and proceeded to clean it up. Then I noticed that no one else's garbage was even touched in their neatly tied Glad bags. The excitement that I felt for these nocturnal hooligans was long gone. It had become their ritual to pile our secrets all over the winding road for every one of our, looking-down-their-nose neighbors to see.

Our hawk was again watching us like same, and he seemed a hell of a lot bigger now that he was perched in a not-so-tall tree, scouring the area for God knows what. The Little Woman returned, from the store, bitching about how the people in California were wandering around the food store in their bare feet and semi-naked attire. She was fed up with their bumping into her and their inconsiderate attitude. I pointed out, "If you look for the bad, that's what you are going to find'. She muttered on, but I dared not tell her about the story just related to me by the Welcomer.

We ate in silence, late in the evening, and heard those furry, nocturnal, scrawny coyotes howling. The next morning we saw roadrunner feathers all over the yard. This was one roadrunner that didn't outsmart Wiley Coyote this time.

The next few days passed with only minor skirmishes. Daughter's number one, two, and three had arrived safely, along with mother, who while circling JFK, held the hand of an elderly fox, to comfort her anxiety.

Early Sunday morning we went to a swap meet. The swap meet can best be described as a hot item flea market. We bought nothing, and were most thankful that we were not assaulted. Upon our return we found a strange car parked in our driveway. I clutched the nightstick I now carried under the front seat, when what to my wondering eyes should appear but the Little Woman's oldest brother. He is in the Army, stationed in Riverside at March AFB. Captain Jack is the biggest, bullshitting, non-stop talking-about-nothing artist in the world. I could tell when he was lying because his mouth was moving. I told the Little Woman so, when I wanted to aggravate her.

He announced that he had little trouble finding the place being as smart as he is; it was easy. They embraced, and I asked meekly, "How long are you going to be here?" He said he had to be back tomorrow night. I sighed a "Thank God". He started to talk and did not stop for eight hours straight. I got in some words like, "I'm sorry, Captain, but I'm going to pull up a floor and catch some shuteye". And I did. I left the Little Woman with brother dear, droning long into the night, and upon awakening I found he was still talking. Now, I'm a pretty good bullshitter, but I'm in kindergarten and this boy is going for his doctorate compared to me. I guess I'm jealous. On he quacked because He didn't even stop while eating. Unbelievable! On and on and on, until it was time to go and command his regiment or whatever the hell he commands. He announced upon leaving that he would not be seeing us again for a while, for he had taken duty to get his next promotion and was going to Turkey. He lied, for he and his Frau stopped back many more times.

After recovering from the voice in my head of Captain Jack and his salty talks, we acquired employment. Dr. Fred's spouse called and said her old college chum was managing a kidney dialysis unit in a hospital in Whittier and would train the Little Woman. The Little Woman has not been employed, save for six months before we got married. Upon marrying, she had given up the idea of working to raise our brood. She had been pregnant a very good portion of our first five years of marriage, and was very shy in the confidence department. I gave her all my professional tips for interviewing and off we went to keep her appointment. It was all for nothing, for she breezed right through. Her physical was set for January first, 1981.

I stumbled into a globetrotting career in a major corporation and within a few days we were both employed. Terrific! We went to the Cask and Cleaver to celebrate. We also called daughters one, two and three and found that no one wanted to come back. Only daughters number two and three returned, reluctantly to put it mildly. When I saw them at LAX at three a.m. Saturday morning, they would not even speak to me except to say, "Get our bags." The drive back was made in dead silence, except for "Please, we would like to sleep." I kept asking "How was this? How was that?" but I finally gave up. However, I did learn that daughter number one was returning with Burly Curly in March.

We also found upon returning, that the Little Woman's bra and slip and my collar pin had reappeared but number one son's Batman Underoos were now missing.

My first assignment was a two-week jaunt that took me to Texas, New Mexico, back to Texas, on to Georgia, north to Virginia and home via O'Hare to LAX. The Little Woman's courage had to be that of a Marine in training for staying in that house alone with her own daughters not even speaking to her—only into a telephone. My admiration for her grew, but I secretly felt she was glad to get rid of me.

We settled into a paycheck-every-two-weeks world. I'm home for two weeks and out two weeks, globe-trotting and working for some privileged punk, who felt he would be president of this corporation by the time he was thirty-five. But I gritted my teeth and bore it, and waited for an opportunity to slide into another division. My relationship with this jerk was going downhill by the moment, and he was trying every which way he could to unload me. I've lived by my wit all my life, and on the day he had finally been given the OK to can me, I transferred out of his trap. Just two hours before this silver spooned fed jerk figured he had me.

Returning from a lengthy trip through the South which found me contending with late flights, lost rental car reservations and missed connections, I returned home via Dallas to LAX on a Friday in late January. After I got to bed and was finally sleeping, our sometimes-working phone rang. It was Mr. Mover. He was in San Bernardino and seeking directions to our home, with our partial shipment of furniture. He said he would be here at eight A.M. but arrived at ten-thirty, with his two burly sons. He demanded his cash or certified check before he unloaded a stick. I had forgotten about that little detail and scoured the house for money. Not enough! "Is the bank open?" I asked, and not waiting for a reply ran down to our bank, while the hawk and the bull both watched me intently. I got enough cash and placed it into his large, calloused hands. His two large sons then unloaded part of our life into our house.

There was not that much coming, so it was easy to see that was missing, the vacuum cleaner, casters for the couch, and the bunk beds. In addition, we acquired a wardrobe box of clothing, that I immediately knew was not ours, but I looked for the possibility it might be the clothes of a wealthy person. I had visions of minks and tweeds, but wouldn't you know, the clothes looked as though they could belong to Red Skelton's Freddie, the Freeloader. I immediately showed my honesty by telling Mr. Mover that the clothes must belong to someone else, for they were not ours. He was not impressed with my honesty, but irritated that he had to move them back onto the truck.

We also noticed four large pillows on our couch were missing. Now picture a sectional with twelve pillows to make the couch, and four missing. Ire makes for uncomfortable sitting. I now explained to Mr. Mover that I wanted my missing items. He looked at me in the saddest, most forlorn and persecuted look he could muster and whined "All of dis here stuff dat is missing will come out of my pockets." For a moment, I almost fell for dis, but caught myself and told him, "I would like to have the claim forms and your notation on the order of the missed items." Reluctantly he conceded and left with number one son and number two sons, or was it number two and number one sons?

We arranged our small lot of furniture and were still considerably short of sleeping quarters since our bunks had not arrived, The Little Woman said, "I'm going to buy more furniture," and off we went to a national store.

Now, when I go car shopping or furniture shopping, in order not to attract any aggressive commission salespeople, I wear my oldest tee shirt and my oldest jeans and the most beat-up pair of sneakers that I can find. They all look at me in disgust, and we are free to roam.

We did for ten minutes this time, until we were spotted by eagle-eyed Chester, who locked onto us like a pitbull in battle and said, "May I help you, Sir?" I got cute, "Help me where?" I said, trying to be obnoxious enough that he would leave me alone. "Across the street? But you don't look like a Boy Scout." I marveled at my wit, but Chester just said with a gleam in his eye, "I'll be here if you need me" He told every salesperson there that we were his, and at the end of every aisle there was Chester, all five ft. four inches of him, watching our every move and gesture. Our pointing at a lamp was his cue to come running. We told him we were just looking. I know the Little Woman and she was just getting warmed up in this delicatessen of lamps, sofas, beds, end tables, coffee tables, and dinettes. It would be at least a six-hour siege before it was over.

Chester ran; Chester walked; Chester matched furniture by running all the way back to the end of the showroom, a distance of about one hundred yards, to get a small end table to match the chair that Chester had just sold the Little Woman. Chester also lifted the sofa bed so that the Little Woman could see the quality and workmanship underneath. After six hours on the nose, Chester had sold twenty four hundred dollars worth of commissionable furniture and was beaming like a Cheshire cat. He was also telling me, almost sobbing, that his wife had just run away with his ex-partner, and he seemed to be eyeing my attractive wife with more than a passing interest.

I signed the contract. We had spent this fine day a total of $3,700, including the moving man and seven dollars and fifty cents for a thick and chewy, at the Pizza Hut.

It was now late February, and I anxiously awaited the arrival of daughter number one and Burly Curly, which was set for late March. In the meantime, daughters number two and three were growing more moody and depressed by the day. Our phone bill had steadily climbed to a healthy $137 per month, so I yanked the phone out of the bedroom where they were secretly making their calls. When they called east they were quieter than two mice pissing in cotton; and the phone bill; as mentioned before, had escalated to monstrous proportions. I consigned the bedroom phone to the garbage, which the coyotes were still strewing throughout the neighborhood.

Things seemed to level off for four or five days when an incident occurred that set the Little Woman and daughters number two and three off the beam again. Also, something was eating or stealing number one son's fish, as four more have now departed. There were now thirty-one. It seems that while daughter number three was walking home from school, a young lad, riding as a passenger in a low rider, took aim on daughter number three's cute little fanny and scored a bulls eye, with the palm of his hand. That hurt her ego more than her fanny. She told this story to the Little Woman, who immediately streaked to our beloved milquetoast staff at our daughter's alma mater. Now, they say that Hell hath no fury like a woman scorned. And the Little Woman is generally level headed and cool, except when two things occur: the harming of one hair on any of her offspring's heads, or an act of incompetence. Both had occurred. We had fought for bus service for our darlings to no avail. The reason being, we lived outside the red line on the map in school and consequently, we were not entitled, according to the Head Milquetoast. The Little Woman would listen to nothing, and stormed into the high school and demanded to see the Head Milquetoast. She would stop at nothing and planned to sleep there until she had seen him. Before I followed her, I called Dr. Fred for the bail money that I felt I was certainly going to need after this was over. When something like this happens, you are somewhat personally hurt, for your flesh and blood has been violated. I was pissed off, too, and settled into the waiting room.

He knew who was there, for he had tangled with the Little Woman before. I felt he would rather walk over a hot bed of coals on his hands, than face what was on the other side of that door. However, he couldn't get out of the windows in his office, for they were barred. He had two choices at this point: tangle with the Little Woman or stay in there forever. He chose the former. As we entered he was smiling a sickly smile and his hands were very wet as he clutched mine in a dead-fish handshake. He said, very weakly, "Now what is the problem?" That was the wrong thing to say, for the Little Woman creamed, "The problem! The problem is you and this place!" "He is the problem", pointing at me, "for bringing me to this Godforsaken hole". What happened was that Head Milquetoast was sinking further into his overstuffed school colored chair and was now terrified, and looking to me for help that I could not give. I've seen her like this before and nothing, I mean nothing, will appease her but results.

He remembered the bus ordeal as the Little Woman related it, and sent for the map. The Little Woman would stop at nothing now, for she was going in for the kill. And Head Milquetoast was scared shitless and wishing he was anywhere but in this land of the golden sun and bodies. As he shook and vibrated the map to the table wrong side up, the Little Woman immediately recognized it as the Southern

California Freeway System, and barked, "That's the wrong side." He immediately flipped it over to the streets of San Dimas, recovered quickly, and said "Where do you live, Mrs. Little Woman?" She pointed quickly for she knew this little map from the bus incident before. Our house was a good inch outside the red fence. Mr. Milquetoast turned even paler than before and submitted. The bus will hereafter pick them up and deliver them to the door, no problem. The Little Woman just looked him dead in the eye and gritted, "It had better!" She then marched out, with me trailing close behind, grateful that I didn't need the bail money. Head Milquetoast felt, I'm sure, that if it were the last thing he did, he'd better not screw this one up.

Fresh from her victory, and gratified by the punctuality of the Uneeda School District, the Little Woman had settled into a relatively serene pattern.

I started globe trotting again, this time off to the great southwest and the lovely town of McAllen, Texas. I arrived on a very late Texas International, and by the time bag and baggage were secure, it was twelve-thirty A.M. CST. As customary, I called home, praying that the phone was working. It rang busy, of course. I checked with my friendly operator who connected me to my friendly repair operator, who almost knew me by name. I knew her daughter had been giving her trouble and asked about her welfare. She replied "She's coming around."

Enough of the pleasantries and down to business. "Are the lines out of order again?" I asked. She rang and said no; there was a conversation going on. I figured it was Super Jock and daughter number three. I was tired, and I had an early appointment, so I told her it was an emergency and to cut in.

The Pomona operator dutifully did this and announced it was clear, go ahead. What I heard was a high-pitched scream, "Please leave me alone. Don't hurt me, please, please, please!!" The woman's voice was pleading with some animal. Now my mind began spinning like a top, and I could not believe what I heard. The line went dead.

Now, I am not sure what I did or thought the next five minutes, but

I went through the same ritual again, only to be told by Pomona Operator Number 2827 that there was trouble on the line. Well, that was all I had to hear. Now my brain could only picture a madman slaughtering, raping, and sodomizing my beautiful family.

I couldn't think; I couldn't reason. I was two thousand miles away and had no possible way of contacting anyone because I didn't know Ferdinand the bull's owner's name, much less his phone number. Anxiety almost overwhelmed me. Finally, the thought process started to work.

I called the San Dimas Police Department and explained calmly that I was on a business trip 2,000 miles away form home. Would they please check on my family, for I cannot get in touch with them. I told them my address, and asked them to give the Little Woman this telephone number to call.

It was now two-thirty a.m. and as I waited for her return call I paced, smoked, paced and smoked for one hour. Still no jingling of my little yellow phone on the nightstand in McAllen, Texas. I was almost crazed with thoughts of blood-splattered walls and our orange rugs.

Finally, I called the Police again. A pleasant sounding voice assured me that my family was fine, and there was no problem; the two officers had done their duty and given her the telephone number. Still there was no call. I couldn't believe that they were unharmed until I heard the Little Woman's voice.

I did not hear that until two pm of the next day, as I kept my business appointment. Actually, I could not have sold whores to an army camp much less this product, to this typical "OK, buddy what's on your mind" client. I called the Little Woman at work after trying many times to contact home again by phone, and I finally heard her voice. Thank God! She told me the Police had been there, and she had called the number many times, but it always came up the same. She kept waking up the same guy somewhere in Texas, and he was getting mighty pissed off at this nonsense, and told her so. We compared numbers later, and they matched perfectly. I don't know who the Little Woman reached, but our lady spirit was playing dirty pool now. I wished she would knock it off since I was so shaken from this experience, I was worthless for the rest of the trip through Louisiana, to St. Louis and home via O'Hare.

The terminal was packed, as I knew it would be, as I'd taken this flight many times. I checked in; smoking aisle please; and boarded the luxurious silver and red monster that would carry me the odd 1,700 miles or so home. I was beat. Finding my seat, I stuffed by briefcase under it, fastened my seat belt, unloosened my tie and tried to fall asleep. A voice sounded, "I stopped traveling in suits a long time ago," it said. Opening one eye, the right one, I noticed a fat, scared-looking individual I'd bet was on the second flight of his life and wanted companionship on the takeoff—someone to hold his hand. Well, I needed someone to hold my whole body at this point, and I was not going to wet nurse any fiftyish jerk who had probably just gotten a luxurious new position filled with glamour. That glamour will wear off soon enough, so I might as well take a chunk out of it right now. I motioned him closer, across the empty seat, to my whispering lips. We had passed the point of no return on the runway and the jumbo was shaking a bit and we were almost airborne. I whispered; you know when the plane shakes like this I really get scared and feel "O My" are we going to crash? I really hated myself for this, but I knew from my glamorous time that this would have shut me up. It certainly worked on this voice. As I recall in between my naps, he did not even eat his overdone fillet mignon. But he sure did smoke and drink the flight away without even looking my way.

We bumped into LAX and home. I was never happier to see anyone than I was to see the Little Woman, daughters number two and three, and number one son. I felt they were almost happy to see me.

I was calling the east now on a regular basis, trying to pry daughter number one from the arms of her old home environment. At last she vowed she would arrive March twenty-fifth, 1981 at LAX from JFK, on Capitol's Super Saver Sky Service. Along with Ma Bell, Capitol Airlines was doing very well.

71

To get daughters number two and three out of their depression and to restore myself to sanity, I had promised against the Little Woman's wishes, to ship them back east for daughter number two's prom. I felt it would be tragic for her to miss it. I should have realized by this time that I was only buying time. It wouldn't be long before we would all depart my land of golden bliss.

They would fly Capitol, of course. They had set their itineraries again. I scolded again. They disbelieved again.

Burly Curly had obtained a seat on the same flight and would be arriving with daughter number one to seek his fortune here also. I OK'd this move, but I needed him with us like Custer needed another Indian at the Little Big Horn.

Big day arrived. Capitol Super Saver Sky Service was to arrive at nine-fifty pm, EST. We also learned from a beaming daughter number three that Super Jock would arrive via Capitol flight JFK/LAX on April fourteenth, 1981. I couldn't believe this. It was getting more ludicrous by the moment. They were all turning into birds.

We were driving on the Santa Monica Freeway to pick up daughter number one and Burly Curly when someone jumped onto the Freeway waving his arms. I swerved and just missed flattening him, but kept right on going to pick up our first-born, who was somewhere out in the heavens over Arizona. We arrived at the International terminal. I felt that after all the money I'd spent, and would spend, Capitol should soon be able to afford their own terminal.

There she was. I spied her with her winter white skin and close cropped blond hair, barking directions at Burly Curly who was loaded down with her paraphernalia—and she does not travel light. Burly Curly was a nervous, well-intentioned youth who was hopelessly in love with daughter number one. He approached me cautiously, admiring my golden skin and light streaked hair. He shouted aloud in the baggage area, "I'm here! I can't believe it! I'm here!"

We fought the crowd, got the luggage, and were headed for the parking lot when Burly Curly spied a palm tree. I thought he was having an ejaculation. A palm tree can do this? Imagine what Disneyland will do.

We settled into our bronze sedan and headed home. Burly Curly was agreeing with everything I said. We arrived home and found daughters number two and three had baked a welcome-home cake for the duo. Burly Curly was enthralled by the view which was exceptionally beautiful that night. We talked and he still agreed with everything I said. He called his mother, who felt I was sure, that she had lost her son to the land of plenty.

I took three days off to prepare for an extra-long trip of three weeks. That would bring me home the same night Super Jock was to arrive to daughter number three's open arms.

Capitol Super Sky Saver flight for daughters number two and three was booked for two p.m., June fourteenth, 1981. That was the day school let out. They were to be dismissed at noon, and I had to have them at LAX by one-thirty p.m. It would be close. They were a bit anxious.

Before I left on my jaunt, daughter number one demanded a dog. Again, to keep her happy I gave in. She was on the phone making arrangements with someone to meet at eight p.m. tonight in the mountains of Riverside. We traveled to the end of the earth, it seemed, to procure this mutt. We were lost many times, but we finally found the mobile home in the middle of nowhere. Here were brown and black pups for daughter number one to choose between. After much deliberation she chose dog number one, "the brown cute one". She paid the squaw five dollars, and after a stop in Riverside to buy puppy chow, a rubber bone and a collar, we were homeward bound.

Before I left, I had to meet with my generous benefactor, who had let me live rent-free for five months, a very noble gesture indeed. I called Dr. Renaldo to meet and discuss rent payment and his plans for our domain. We arranged to meet at a local hospital. After my ninth try, I finally caught him at a not-so-surprising place, a bank. Dr. Renaldo Arrigga was a multi-millionaire and a slick businessman— as I was about to find out. We met, and he smiled that closed-eyed smile of his, and we talked. I always respect direct conversation, and when I ask direct questions I expect direct answers. I asked "How much do you want per month for us to live there?" He said, "Uh, well, how much do you want to pay?" Damn it! He answered a question with a question—a bad start. How much do I want to pay? I think exactly what I'm paying now-zero, zilch, nothing. I felt sorry for Dr. Fred, for he was embarrassed. I asked again, and he finally said $650 per month starting April first, 1981. I agreed. My only concerns at this point were two things: how I would tell the Little Woman that we were paying $650 for a place that was haunted and which she hated; and how long was he planning on allowing us to stay there. He smiled that closed eye smile, and said, "As long as you want to." He would not sell that place for anything, for he loved it dearly. If he did ever sell it, I would get first shot at it.

I believed this. I thanked him and left. I went home and opened the door. She greeted me with "How much?" I said "$650 per month starting April first, 1981." I watched her mouth open to scream, and I hastily excused myself to go out for cigarettes until she had calmed down. I had anticipated this so I hadn't even turned the engine off. She was still screaming as I drove down the hill and the car lights caught Ferdinand's eyes. The Little Woman started right up where she had left off two hours later when I returned. I headed straight to bed and stepped in puppy shit in the bathroom. The little puppy was sleeping in his box, and I noticed a little twitch as I passed.

The puppy had cost daughter number one sixty-five dollars so far; puppy chow, shot for this, shots for that, a pill for this, a pill for that, and he had not yet been with us for two days. Nothing but the best for this puppy.

I left on my extended trip from LAX to Denver, Dallas and Atlanta. In Minneapolis my rental car had a flat tire. In Bloomington there was a big hassle. On to Cleveland, "the mistake on the lake" to a wrong motel. To Baltimore-Washington, and Birmingham (I couldn't understand a soul there) and to boot, I had my watch lifted in the motel. From New Orleans onto Phoenix and back to LAX. All in all it was a successful trip. I sold some product and was propositioned twice, but declined, and had no phone problems.

Super Jock had arrived ahead of me and was already cuddled into the arms of my glowing daughter number three. I started his evening off right by asking "How long are you staying?" "Three weeks" he replied. "Three weeks! Holy Hell!" I stumbled to bed past the puppy that was now twitching very badly. Daughter number one was crying, for they had already contacted the vet who suggested that we put the dog away. It had distemper and must be destroyed. Tomorrow. "Lord," I muttered. "Can't anything go right?" And, "Watch it, lady spirit." Burly Curly was now insisting that he had been seeing objects late at night. We hadn't told him about our teenage spirit, but explained it was the mirrors.

Super Jock and Burly Curly were floating around the house in seventh heaven. Burly Curly found employment finally, only three blocks down the hill. He could walk it, which was great to me.

Dr. Fred came to visit with his spouse and sons Martin and Manuel. We were talking about old times, and he started to relate a story it to me.

It seems that there is a tribe known as the Negritos in the country where Clark Air Force Base is located. Before Clark, the Negritos had owned the land that the U.S. took away, and in return had given the tribe of Negritos free hospitalization until the last Negrito has gone to that big jungle in the sky. According to Dr. Fred the largest Negrito was about forty-two inches high and weighed about sixty-five lbs. From the way Dr. Fred explained it, the Negritos were very primitive and independent in their survival. They are reluctant to seek any assistance at all, even when close to death.

It seems that one fine day a group of Negritos were hunting dinner, when a good-sized bevy of quail appeared overhead. They were hunting with blowguns, and one Negrito puffed and blew a bulls eye hit right through the heart of an unlucky quail. While other Negritos watched, looking up in admiration, the blow dart and quail fell back to earth—the point of the dart with the quail on it struck the watching Negritos' forehead. The Negritos rallied around the fallen warrior and were trying to pull the dart from their comrade's forehead, but to no avail. What should they do? The Queen Negrito ordered them to the hospital where Dr. Fred was wading through vaccinations and polio shots that no one really wanted, when the band of savages appeared. Dr. Fred, a linguist who spoke their language, wheedled out of the Queen why this Negrito had a dart with a quail on it sticking a half inch into his skull. The main concerns of the tribe were as follows: to get the quail off the dart for dinner; to get the dart back for it would take much labor to make another; to get back to hunting; and, if possible, to get medical attention for the warrior.

Dr. Fred explained that they would have to x-ray and surgically remove the dart. No dice. The Negrito Queen wanted the quail and the dart, and she wanted it now. All the while the little brown pigmy was flashing his eyes around and seeing his tribe's concern for him faltering, decided to run. And run he did, through the hospital and into the jungle, presumably tired of all this shit. He probably took the dart and the quail out, and ate the quail himself. In any case, it was the last time Dr. Fred saw him.

I was hysterical at this amusing story. It was about then that Martin threw Manuel into our fish pond and Manuel came in dripping wet in his seventy-five dollar baby suit. Dr. Fred packed them up and left.

Daughter number one was quite sad. They had put her puppy away. Burly Curly was getting nothing but snide remarks from her, but Super Jock was in heaven, being waited on hand and foot by daughter number three. It seemed, from his conversation with his mother, that his family was quite disappointed, really pissed off, that he was still in the Golden State. He had already missed two games of baseball, and the coach was wondering whether the disease that he had was fatal. "Yes it is" I remarked, "terminal heat". This received dirty looks from everyone.

I noticed that Burly Curly and daughter number one's love for each other was fading, for they were sniping and arguing. Daughter number one came to dear old Dad and ordered, "You (meaning me) have to get rid of him."

"I have to get rid of him? You brought him here."

"What the hell do you mean?" She had decided that it would be better if they separated as their relationship was stagnating. I was listening in disbelief to this sad tale, but firmly told her, "If you want him out, you get him out. Tell him to go to the 'Y' or somewhere."

Now, Burly Curly, as mentioned before, has arms bigger around than my waist, as might be expected for an All-State wrestler. There was no way that I was going to tangle with him. We argued, and she said she would try to get along. I said "You'd better."

Super Jock and daughter number three were in a state of divine bliss, billing and cooing.

Daughter number two had blended in with the décor and was getting straight A's and on the State Honor Roll. She was staying out of the mainstream of life, and I was concerned about her.

The days were drifting by, and it was now May first, 1981. The girls were now down to forty-five pennies in the jar, which signified the number of days left in California until summer departure to the great northeast.

One evening I fell fast asleep on the couch watching TV, when something awakened me in the silent room. Seeing an image with my sleep filled eyes, I thought it was the Little Woman coming out of the bedroom to bring me to our love nest. I remember thinking, "But wait, since when does the Little Woman wear saddle shoes and pedal pushers and thick wool socks? She hasn't worn those since I was trying to take them off her, to no avail, in our courting days." I looked up to see the face, and what I saw was an alabaster, non-featured head atop a very square pair of shoulders. I tried to speak, and the image was gone. Call it a dream, call it a hallucination. Call it whatever. I now call it our little murdered teenager. I bolted for the bedroom and did not relate this tale for a full year after it happened. You may call me crazy, and I know I was under great pressure during this period, but I do know what I saw.

The next day, daughter number three couldn't find her new bathing suit, and my son's underoos had returned. I was now convinced that we were haunted by that unsolved murder victim— the poor unrested wandering spirit. I had to find out about this murder by going to the Pomona Library.

I went to check the microfilm from every daily newspaper from 1955 to 1959. It was pure misery after March 1958, and my eyesight was failing from reading every line of microfilm I found. I preferred not to go blind, so I dismissed this venture. I called on the man who had related the tale of the murder to me, but it seemed he did not exist. I went to see if the check, I had written him, had come back, so I could get his name. You guessed it. I couldn't find the check.

Enough of the lady poltergeist and on with my existence. Another trip of one week. The phone worked one day out of four, and I fixed it from Louisville with my friendly repair operator's assistance. Burly Curly and daughter number one were now openly battling, and I told him he must go. He pleaded, and I relented.

The day came for Super Jock to sprout wings and return home. I couldn't bear any more sorrow, so I instructed daughter number two to take him to LAX since I was taking number one son and wife to San Diego for the day to see the Padres play at Jack Murphy Stadium. We enjoyed the drive and the game, and returned to daughter number three's sorrow with daughter number two consoling her reassuringly, that there were only thirty-nine days to go, and she would be back in his arms again.

Burly Curly and daughter number one were fighting relentlessly now. It was a constant thing, and I felt I would probably go mad shortly.

What the hell! Daughter number three's bathing suit returned, and the Little Woman's curlers and lipstick were now misplaced. Looked as though the spirit was getting ready to go to the prom.

I looked to the corral and noticed something different. All that was left of Ferdinand were his entrails. He had been slaughtered and was flash-frozen in red chunks somewhere in a freezer. The neighbor asked if I would like a roast, but I declined politely, I just couldn't, thank you.

Number one son was crying for Ferddy. They had been getting along pretty well of late. He was down to twenty-four fish now, as Manuel's flop in the pond must have wounded some.

It was time to get the sedan registered in California. I had been driving around for six months with a cardboard temporary

Pennsylvania plate. We had bought the car just before our trip west, and I had not paid any sales tax. Any state will frown upon this, not to mention the lending institution that was holding the lien on the car; they wanted their title. So, I went to DMV in Pomona to a line that was four blocks long and growing by the minute. It was nine am and 105 degrees. Don't let anyone tell you it is not hot because it is dry heat—I say that 105 degrees is hot! However, it was more sun to tan with to, which add to my already golden glow. Finally, I was goldened out when I reached inside at eleven A.M. Just a short two hours more and I was standing before the DMV man. I claimed to have just arrived in California and was doing my duty to register and pay sales tax on said vehicle. He took all the necessary paperwork and said not a word until he itemized: $666 in sales tax; $175 for California registration fee; forty-two dollars for driving privileges; and the car had not yet been certified for the smog and pollution test, which for sure, would be at least another fifty dollars. Total $943! "Pay the cashier" the DMV man said. What! I don't have that much money on me. "You should have called first."

"Yes," I agreed. "But we don't have a phone yet" I lied. "Certainly there must be something we can work out." DMV man said, "Damn, everyone comes here thinking its milk and honey! It costs bread to live in this Golden State." I had been tied up here for four and a half hours, and I was going to get something for my time. He finally decided that for the registration for of $175, and forty-two dollars for driving privilege, he would give me a sixty-day extension, good till July sixteenth, 1981. I gladly forked over the money to the cashier and got my little red two-month pass. I never did register that car in California. One year later, the cardboard license was so gasoline stained and deteriorated that no one could even recognize the state it was from. I procured my red pass by jumping from city to city every sixty days, to explain to the DMV man or woman, that we had just moved here and I didn't have the sales tax, for the Little Woman had returned from back east, and had finally decided she couldn't live without me. This had put me in a terrible financial fix. It may sound stupid, but it worked every time. I always got that little red, moistened-along-the-edges-and-display-in-right-corner-of-window, two-month pass. I never did pay any more fees to the Golden State. I skirted my duty, and now I am sorry; but, survival is survival. Many thanks to the lending institution (you know who you are) for helping me through this trying time—though you did threaten me once or twice, didn't you?

The Little Woman was sewing in the dining room one evening, and looking up to square her eyes away, she noticed an image. After much questioning by me, she said the image was dressed exactly as I had seen her dressed. Now, you will remember, I did not tell my tale to anyone at all. Yet, the Little Woman's account was identical to what I had seen: saddle shoes, pony tail, pedal pushers, wool socks; only that night she was wearing a blouse with a Peter Pan collar. Believe me, my Little Woman does not lie, exaggerate or embellish a story, as I have been accused of doing on occasion. Now I knew that my evening on the couch was not due to pressure, nor was it hallucination. She must really exist; at least her spirit does.

The situation became grave after this sighting. The Little Woman was now peeking around corners and looking under furniture. She wanted out, and wanted out now. So, when the underhanded sawbones (my landlord) was gathering his prospects to dump my not-so-rent-nor-spirit-free-home, the Little Woman was not too unhappy at all.

I was now awakened by various odd sized Orientals ringing our bell and running around the place as though they owned it. They shortly would. Dr. Arrigga obviously didn't love this place as much as he said he did, or his love for cash was much greater. The little humanitarian was obviously selling it to one of the three little, brown, smiling bantams who exclaimed, "Rook at the rizards'" "What a biew." I tried to call Dr. Renaldo, to no avail. He would not return my calls. So, now I would not return his rent. I was fed up with all this nonsense, but logic told me I had asked for it—every inch of it.

I began making plans to move when his letter arrived stating that we were to vacate the premises by June thirtieth, 1981. I sent the rent and started vacating, boxing, looking, and looking, and looking.

I contacted a multitude of realtors in the area we chose. I finally settled on one Sherman Nearsworth, sixtyish and a nice guy, but who had a very annoying manner of speech. He would talk for a while in a dry, professional monotone and then, without any warning raise his voice to a monstrously high level and said that finding a place in the places that I had designated would be VERY EXPENSIVE. Was I prepared to pay $800-$1200 per month to rent one of these homes in Orange County? Of course, I was not prepared to pay that kind of rent, but what was I going to do? June thirtieth was the last day that I could live in my rent-free cottage, and I had no other choice unless I wanted to live in the Barrio's. We ventured forth on a fine sunny day in May to look at six promising rentals. They were all dumps with prices ranging from $750-$1000 per month.

The Little Woman had mixed emotions. She was only too glad to leave our stench-filled, spirit house, but she was getting ill from looking at this junk that Mr. Nearsworth was showing us. She wanted only to leave and go back east immediately. I was still selling them on California. Why, I don't know. It was stubbornness, I assume. Or, a very sick mind.

Burly Curly and daughter number one's relationship had worsened to the point of her agitating him to the brink of trying to take a swipe at her. "That's it" I shouted. "I don't take swipes at my offspring, and certainly no in-heat beau is going to!" I told him to get the hell out on the next available flight east, west, north or south, or stay in California. I don't give a damn, just go. He made arrangements for departure on June seventh, 1981, via Capitol Super Saver to JFK. Now, I am patient and understanding, but no way would I allow someone, whom we were feeding and housing, to take the liberties that Burly Curly had. Daughter number one compared me to Pontius Pilate, as did daughters two and three.

Mr. Nearsworth called and said there were more homes to see that he felt we would like, AND WOULD LIKE to know if we could meet him near Disneyland at one pm. I agreed. More dumps which we declined.

Time was getting short for dismissal day at school, and the girls were packed and ready to board their Capitol flight to JFK. Daughter number three whispered in my ear with a husky voice, "Thank you, Dad." They were off. I felt like crying and did.

Daughter number one was sulking and writing to Burly Curly

when I returned. Number one son was now sad because he was down to eighteen fish. He would not let them go when we moved, and I had no idea what I was going to do with them, for it was almost certain that we would not find a house by D-Day II. We'd probably have to seek refuge in a motel. I was unable to inflict any more sorrow on the ones I love, and I feared for my sanity.

To add to the already near-disastrous situation, I received a registered and certified letter from Mr. Mover regarding the bulk of my furniture, which was still in storage. I had never received a storage bill, but the letter stated that under ICC Rule Number such and such, he was going to sell all my worldlies if I did not respond to this letter within ten days. I owed him $500 for storage. I got on the phone and worked out an agreement to pay monthly. He said it was OK but he'd better see some dough soon. When we left I had given him Dr. Fred's address, but Dr. Fred's spouse had not forwarded the mail, nor the Texas International Airlines request for an interview with daughter number one. This had been a life long dream for her, and now the lady spirit was really playing dirty pool. This certainly didn't help matters, as time had elapsed, the interview was three weeks ago.

The Little Woman was now frantic and once again on a downhill slide. Mr. Nearsworth was calling on a regular basis, and I knew June thirtieth was rapidly approaching. I was ready to rent a garage by now, but the Little Woman was quite a bit more selective, so we persevered. Daughter number one was very unhappy and threatened to leave us for good. She settled for two weeks with friends just to get away from us, after the mail debacle.

Success! We found a house in Anaheim to our liking, but the renter didn't like us. Mr. Nearsworth and I had to very strongly sell Mrs. Renter. After a week of phone calls and waving of cold cash under her nose, she finally gave in. It seems she was leaving California to marry in Wisconsin. However, she would not leave until July ninth. That left a gap of nine days. I would have to motel hunt now, and store our newly acquired furniture again. This was really becoming a pain in the ass, this quest for happiness in the now, not-so-golden land of opportunity.

The lease was finally signed on the twenty-eighth of June. On to the movers again, to move and store. It seems the good doctor found two real fish in the persons of Dr. and Mrs. Boomewong, or something like that. Mrs. Boomerwong was three feet ten inches tall, fat and unable to speak English very well. Dr. Boomerwong was tall, thin and gullible for they shelled out $200,000 for my dream house. They were anxious to move in. I let them, on June twenty-ninth, at three p.m. right after the movers had gone.

Our little spirit had given us a going away party. The lights were blinking constantly, and the stench had returned worse than ever. A lamp on the wall had fallen to the floor for no apparent reason.

The Little Woman and I were again close to divorce, and three more fish had disappeared. Now what would I do with the remaining fish? I couldn't break my little boy's heart. I called Mel's, at the fish shop where they were purchased, and asked if he would board the fish. He said it was very unusual, but since I was wacky enough to make this request, he would be just as wacky and board them for two dollars, for the ten days. At last something had gone right! We moved that very day into a motel. I said goodbye to the lady spirit, and she said goodbye with our tire going flat upon our departure.

Now we had to mark time in this motel that cost forty-five dollars per evening. I had to find something cheaper quick.

Enter a small South Korean by the name of Wun Sun from Taejon. He was friendly, and it appeared that he would negotiate. I asked Mr. Wun Sun how much it would be for a stay of nine days. He said thirty-six fifty per night, but a special rate of thirty-four dollars would apply. "Too much" I said, and started to walk out when I noticed a worn pair of sneakers on his little feet. I had a pair of Nikes that had been given to me, but were too small and thus, never worn. I went to the sedan and rummaged them out of the trunk. Wun Sun liked what he saw, so I said twenty-eight dollars per night and the sneakers are yours." He wanted to badly, but was afraid of his boss and declined. I had also noticed that his pants were frayed. I told number one son to grab two pair of pants that I never wore because they didn't fit. Wun Sun couldn't resist and said "We have a deal."

He cautioned us not to tell anyone for he would certainly "roose" his job. I agreed, and we moved into our new house with the famous Pine Tree for which the motel was aptly named.

For the next 260 hours or until Mrs. Renter decided when to get the hell out, this was our home. I fearing, that Mrs. Renter might get cold feet about giving her hand and body in marriage, and I hoped she wouldn't chicken out. The Little Woman was so very happy to be out of our dream house that the days sped by swiftly. Soon we had only five days left.

That day, for the use of the motel's laundry, I gave Harry, as I was calling him now, a shirt I never wore, and he threw in coffee in the mornings, and the use of the pool after hours. It made me feel almost like a celebrity. I threw in some free product from my company, and Harry made sure we had an extra ration of soap and towels. Mrs. Harry made us her favorite South Korean dish. I didn't know what it was, but it had been buried in their backyard for two weeks before serving. I knew the South Koreans ate a lot of dog meat. Harry wanted very badly to tell me, but I didn't want to know. Whatever it was, it was meat wrapped in leaves, and that was enough for me to know.

Harry was sorry to see us leave, and I noticed a tear in his eye as I was signing the American Express receipt, that bailed us out of the Famous Pine Tree. Mrs. Renter's fiancé must have finally sold her on matrimony, as she had flown to Wisconsin to marry her suitor, much to my relief I called Mr. Mover again to cart our worldlies to Anaheim and our new residence.

The Last Leg

It looked like the Little Woman might make it now that we were free of our little spirit, and it appeared that she liked our new home. So, I said, "Let's leave all that past shit behind and start anew."

Daughter number one seemed somewhat happy with our new home, which was quite nice, and she had just landed a fairly good job at JCPenney and was making plans for college in the fall. I called daughters numbers two and three and they seemed anxious to fly back in August. Daughter number two's prom had gone very well. And number one son had his fish back. This time they were in an aquarium that he and I had bought at a yard sale, from two rather tipsy men who had let filter, aquarium, rocks and fish food go for two dollars and fifty cents. Things were quiet and seemed to be stabilizing. Maybe it was the spirit, we said. Everyone seemed happy, and I could almost relax and pay attention to my livelihood for a change.

The Little Woman agreed to give Southern California one more try and really overlook all the things that had pissed her off in the past about the Land of Opportunity. I was promoted again, really moving up the ladder, I though proudly. Everything seemed better. I had high hopes once more.

The Little Woman was rearranging the house, something she hadn't done since we landed. I felt this was a very healthy sign. Daughter number one was really aggressively selling the new environment to daughters two and three. They were somewhat skeptical, but would sooner believe their sister than their father. They were going to return in three weeks. Number one son's aquarium was really pretty in our new living room. Daughter number one had captured the upstairs bath and was planning on not letting her sisters in when they returned.

I was becoming quite happy because everyone else was happy. Our social life was expanding as we acquired a new set of friends, all purely social. Social, except for Lois, a cute little midwestern farm girl who, since arriving in California, apparently had been trying to ball everything with pants on, from what I could see, she was succeeding. So, the Little Woman was watching me like a hawk. She need not have bothered. Balling Lois was the farthest thing from my now almost-serene skull.

We met Ronald and Uri, two of the finest people I have ever met in my life. They have one little boy, Mark and one little girl, Akiah, the prettiest Eurasian beauty I have ever seen. This was a real pleasurable experience. Both were educated and good people, with Yuri being as gentle as a lotus flower and just as pretty. Ronald, I know you read only non-fiction, but I hope you are reading this so I can say "Thank you, both, for everything.

We were a family again. Daughters number two and three returned exclaiming that they loved the house. They told of all their experiences, good and bad, and how the Capitol Super Saver flight was great. DC-ten service this time. They were really going to try to adjust and help me to establish Southern California as our home. Number one son procured a small paper route through our neighborhood. We also learned that a family of three girls and one boy had moved in one block from us. Daughters number one, two, and three were the same ages as those little darlings from Syracuse, New York. "This should make it much easier in their adjustment," I said, and everyone agreed. Things were delightful. The girls no longer locked themselves in their rooms. They were actually even eating dinner with us. We were a family again, for the first time since my announcement of our trek to the Land of Opportunity.

We received a phone call one fine August day. To my delight and that of the Little Woman, it was her best friend form home, Mary, and her husband, Richard. They were in, of all places, Los Angeles and would like to visit, if we wouldn't mind. If we wouldn't mind! To get them here I would have gladly carried them both on my back on the freeway for it could do nothing but good for the Little Woman. This was too good to be true. They arrived at six pm and insisted on taking us out to dinner. I couldn't believe this. It was too good to be true. We ate with Mary and the Little Woman just beaming and talking. Rich and I got along fairly well. All in all, it was a delightful evening that I wished would never end.

It seemed they were taking their oldest son back to college. I had come to understand from the Little Woman that, compared to him, George Will is a slow learner. I almost begged them to stay over, but they had to go. We invited them back for dinner the next evening and they agreed. I noticed the Little Woman's eyes, and I didn't like the forlorn, homesick look that I saw. I hoped this would pass, for the visit could go either way. With great expectations I awaited our dinner engagement with Rich and Mary the following night.

I saw it starting all over again the next day when the Little Woman returned from paying sixty-five dollars for a filling in number one son's baby tooth. Burly Curly and Super Jock were ringing our phone off the wall (during this period the phone was working). Mary and Rich arrived after depositing their oldest son at college. We ate and chatted. I noticed the fire in the Little Woman's eyes as she related tales of our life in the Golden state so far. What she was relating was not good. It was then I knew again, it would never work. Her dislike for Southern California, with all its glory, was too strong for me to overcome in my already beaten condition. I was defeated after being worked over by four females that I love dearly.

Rich and Mary had to go. They were leaving the next day. As they drove their rental car away a lot of the Little Woman went with them. I now know things were on the decline after the Little Woman seeing her best friend. I had known it could go either way, and it did—the wrong way.

The smog in August can only be described as smoggy. It didn't bother me too much since I am a smoker and probably my lungs, with the tar and nicotine, made quick work of the offending smog.

However, it did bother daughter number one very much, and we were at the hospital with her many times. Every time it was the same prescription, move back east. This was the recommendation from all those noteworthy California physicians.

The relationship between daughters number, one, two and three and the gals from Syracuse declined. My offspring had stated that those little ladies would have no problem adjusting since they loved smoking dope and orgies.

I knew then that my family was not suited for this Sodom and Gomorrah. My thinking had done a complete 180-degree turnaround. It had only taken nine months. The wife was complaining that is seemed every lady she knew of her age had had one, two, three and even four abortions, and they though nothing of it. It appalled her.

The Little Woman was invited to a "Naughty Lady party by one of her acquaintances at the unit where she was still reluctantly working. Not knowing what this was about, she declined—she is no one's fool. But she was inquisitive enough the next day to ask about it. This event was described by her yoga, vegetarian dietician Kitty Lee. It seems that all the ladies are invited to one's home, and the gals all kick in for a male dancer from a famous Los Angeles nightclub. He does his thing—dancing bare ass among this sea of married and unmarried females. The bravest of the bunch rub this gentleman down with exotic creams and perfumes; and I imagine, at this time passion and booze are flowing fairly well as a few ladies jump this fellow's bones and ball him. The grand finale was done by only the bravest and sexiest, for she orally copulated with the exotic male dancer in full view, to the delight of the other wenches. The Little Woman related this to me, and this one greatly alarmed me for some of these "Naughty Ladies" had their offspring with them.

I assume the male dancer was fairly bushed after this event, for believe it or not; he got paid again by those "Naughty Ladies." Talk about the best of all possible worlds! This boy had quite a position. If I sound jealous, I probably am. Save for one thing: I would always wonder about who I kiss after that.

We hadn't met any of our neighbor's yet, but one day the bell rang and it was our first encounter with Irving Eureen. He had noticed that we hadn't trimmed our lawn yet. I knew he was trying to make a buck by shaming me into buying his lawnmower. My first instinct was to slam the door in his face, but I listened to his pitch and restrained myself and declined. Irving was the type of fellow with mod glasses and cigarette holder who thinks he looks forty, but is actually sixty-five. I invited him in. He immediately asked, as he eyed the Little Woman and daughters number one, two and three, "How old do you think I am?" Right on schedule I thought. The Little Woman is about to utter the truth, but I shouted over her, "forty-four to forty-eight tops". You never know when you will need someone. Irving smiled and beamed. He was now mine. He let me in on all the little secrets of life and became very entertaining. He claimed that among many other talents, he also could read and analyze handwriting. He wasn't too crazy about reading and analyzing male handwriting, but leaned toward that of females. I pegged him for a potential child and woman molester. It turned out he wasn't for he secretly confided to me much later that he loved to masturbate and fantasize as much as he could.

He analyzed all my female's handwriting, much to the annoyance of all concerned. If he were trying to make points with the ladies, he didn't for he told them they were vain, and selfish. I couldn't believe all this, remembering the smooth operator that had appeared at my door three hours earlier. The females scattered, very angry at this sex symbol, Irving Eureen. Irving and I chatted alone. I still declined his offer on the lawn mower. As he exclaimed that the neighbors frown on non-edged lawns, I told him "I will acquire a gardener."

He left, but was to return many times in the next ten months of our stay. I always welcomed Irving for he always gave me little things to use and books to read, and I really did like the man. However, at times, I felt he was a monstrous pain in the ass. I took that back immediately after he gave me, religiously, every Sunday that the Rams were home, four free tickets to the games at Anaheim Stadium. How I ask can you not like a man like that?

The Little Woman closeted herself every time Irving appeared. She didn't trust him one bit. When I was globetrotting, she always expected him to pay a visit. But Irving never did appear—much to the

Little Woman's apprehension because she was always dreading that he would.

We now experienced an incident that made us natives in twenty seconds. That's how long it took the "Roller" to register five point nine on the Richter scale. It was frightening, to say the least, but somewhat exciting. It had the Little Woman saying that no way would she allow another one of those to take place. In her mood, I believed her. Everyone was upset at every noise for days because radio and TV men kept saying that the after-shock would be greater than the quake itself.

This incident did not enhance my chances for staying in the land of opportunity, for I now saw the Little Woman removing pennies from a jar. I was afraid to ask how many she had started with. To me it looked like about nine months worth and the pile was steadily declining.

We rumbled through August and September in the grips of the worst family feuds I have ever encountered. There were horrible scenes and language, and we came close to inflicting harm. Everyone, including me, couldn't take this anymore. But I continued to fight, to stay and fight.

Daughter number one was enrolled in college, and daughters number two and three were enrolled at the local high school. Number one son was enrolled at the local elementary school, with a fine, intelligent and sensitive sixth grade teacher who openly admitted that California public schools leave something to be desired. He immediately gained the admiration of the Little Woman. A great man—I like him.

I was still living in airports and on airplanes, and now logging more air miles than most stewardesses and seeing some cities over and over. I had made friends in almost every state in the Union.

Burly Curly was phoning regularly, and so was Super Jock. It seemed their love would not die. Super Jock announced has was sprouting wings again and flying Capitol JFK to LAX on December sixteenth, 1981. He already had his ticket, and it was only October.

One day a the office, a disheartened employee announced to

everyone within earshot that he had had enough of this shit. He them leaped through a window four desks away. Since we were only on the third floor, he survived. Everyone commented, with no empathy that he should have at least taken the elevator to the seventh or eighth floor so he could have succeeded in his flight. I found myself almost agreeing with them, but caught myself quickly and regained my sanity.

Halloween back east is a day for the kids to dress up as goblins and ghosts, and to proclaim "Trick or Treat" at your door. Not so in this Land of Fruits and Nuts, as I now refer to it. I think that the constant sun and heat fried everyone's brain. The doorstep was full of goblins and pornographic adults "Trick or Treating". After the first onslaught we left for the evening to find, hopefully, alive and well, number one son, who was apparently doing well in his quest for candy and such. He reluctantly rode with us as I checked his bounty for razor blades and thorns—and I found none.

The arguments between the Little Woman and me were turning into violent scenes, and yet I insisted on staying. God only knows why! I was still hoping against hope that all of the nonsense would disappear, and we could all be a happy family again. I abhorred the thoughts of another holiday for I knew the sadness that it would bring to all. However, I made up my mind to by positive about this and try to make everyone else positive. I failed. They vacillated between misery and homesickness. "I will not give up" I muttered.

We traveled to Disneyland again, to do Frontierland, Tomorrow Land and Adventure Land. We returned home to daughters number one, two and three locked into their rooms not even looking at me again, much less speaking. I sulked on our couch and surveyed a very sad household. The guilt overwhelmed me, and I cried as I felt I had lost all that was near and dear—my lovely family. Only number one son understood and said "Things will be better in the morning, Dad".

I decided that part of the disharmony was due to the diamond earrings that daughter number one was still wearing. We all agreed that they certainly must have something to do with our unhappiness. I told daughter number one to hand them over and much arguing ensued, for this cutie's love for diamonds goes deep. Her idea of something better than a diamond is another diamond. Finally she obeyed. The Little Woman dismounted the diamonds from the posts, and I took them myself. I was leaving Sunday for a week. I would cleverly deposit those infernal rocks as far apart form us as I could. I deposited one gem in the butt can in the DFW airport, and later the other in the Greater Cincinnati airport in Covington, KY. (My apologies to these two cities.)

Burly Curly broke his old record of $210 calling number one daughter, and Super Jock gave him a better run.

Irving Eureen from across the cul-de-sac was here again, drinking coffee, telling me about his latest invention, a revolutionary toilet paper holder that he had just designed, and dropped off four ducats for the Rams-49ers game on Sunday. I was now paying rapt and undivided attention to this man. No one at all could figure out how I was getting these delectable seats, not even the most influential Southern Californians that I knew, could get them. They all felt that the real test, though would be the Monday night game with Atlanta. I just smiled and said "No problem". You see, Irving Eureen hated football. Why he spent this amount of money on something he hated just to give the tickets to me I could never understand. Mine was not to reason why; mine was to watch the football fly. That was exactly what I did every Sunday that the Los Angeles Rams were battering themselves around, for my pleasure, on those fine sunny afternoons in Anaheim Stadium. The procuring of these tickets did begin to lose its prestige as the Rams were getting their butts kicked on a regular basis. I was seeing Rams 1982 season tickets for sale by disgruntled fans in the arena; but I was still quite smug and basked in the arrangement.

If you have been paying attention to my babbling account at all, you will remember Mr. Welcomer, the pilot, who fleeced me out of five dollars. He told me the tale of the murder of the teenage girl, and how he used to fly over the spot where our haunted house was to be built twenty-five years ago. Well, I was sitting in my favorite ham-and –over-easy-eggs restaurant in San Dimas one warm November morning reading the newspaper when a small article caught me eye. It said a certain airport was celebrating its fifteenth anniversary on Saturday. I read on and found that this was the same airport that our rent-free home had overlooked. It didn't hit me immediately that Mr. Welcomer had mentioned that he had flown over this spot twenty-five years ago, out of that very airport. I quickly subtracted fifteen from eighty-one and get 1966, ten years after Mr. Welcomer said he had flown out of the very airport, I was reading about. I thought that the airport must have been under another name before, and read on. All I came up with was the same: it flew its first Piper Cub fifteen years ago, and they were celebrating it Saturday. I looked around the restaurant for a native. They are not hard to spot. They all have dried and tanned leather where flesh should be. I found one, six stools from me. "Pardon me" I said. "This article I am reading says that the airport is celebrating its fifteenth birthday this year. Is it possible that it was under another name prior to that?" Tanned native looked me over and said "not to my knowledge". Before that he recalled strawberry fields and trees. He must have noticed the fright in my eyes, because he asked his buddy native to add that he recalled the same landscape until they started building the airport sixteen years ago.

I was chilled again. Questions arose in my mind: "Why me?" "Who the hell was Mr. Welcomer?" "Did he even exist?" "Why did he even tell me a story like this?" Again, I did not tell the Little Woman or anyone else of this tale. Could all of this have been my imagination or hallucinations? These strange events are continuing to unfold. I couldn't believe it!

I drove to Hollywood's Freak show on business, but I was not paying any attention to Mr. Western Madison Avenue's pitch as to how he would turn my division around with his well-placed TV and newspaper ads. He had already shown me that he had the best credentials in the business. It was nice being the buyer and not the seller for a change. I told him I would let him know and left his office.

A young, blue-jeaned male was urinating on the sidewalk. No one noticed, so why should I? I drove via the Santa Monica to the 605 and

Riverside Freeway home and did not even get lost. This was the first time since we had been here that I hadn't.

Thanksgiving came and went compete with depression and an eight-teen pound turkey. The turkey didn't even take the sting out of our genuine homesickness, for the holidays. I can't explain the feeling, but those of you who have been in this situation will know what I mean.

Super Jock had been calling on a regular basis again, anticipating his arrival in mid-December to spend one month with us. Daughter number three was ecstatic. His impending visit also seemed to brighten the Little Woman's spirits. So the Christmas season started, but with sun shining and palms swaying—no snow, no yule log, no sleigh bells! I was bitching regularly now about the lack of a real Christmas. The Little Woman snapped immediately, "This is what you asked for, so knock it off." The lack of "Christmas" in Christmas was one thing I just couldn't get used to.

The phone rang and the Little Woman answered it and motioned me to the phone. I picked up and heard mother's voice. It seemed she was at a dinner three days ago and missed the first step of the twenty-six steps, and fell the length of the stairs. She wound up with a bump on her head and a minor gash on her femur. I couldn't believe she was OK; she was now seventy-seven. To take a trip down twenty-six marble steps and not break even a finger is a major miracle. Sister Alice, gathering from the conversation that I didn't believe mother, got on the phone and reassured me that mother was fine and had no broken bones. It was a miracle. I could tell from Alice's cool talk that she was not lying to me. It has to be very hard to convince someone 3,000 miles away that his seventy-seven year-old Mother has just fallen down twenty-six marble steps but is all right. I called mother on a daily basis for one week before I was convinced that she was OK. I then dismissed from my mind the picture of my mother in a body cast.

Daughter number two had finally condescended to date one of the many California lads who had begged for just one evening with her. The lucky lad was a tall, lean, dark handsome lad of nineteen by the name of Ryan. We invited him for dinner one evening, and he accepted. As he ate he was constantly throwing salt over his shoulder and blessing himself after each morsel. Now, I knew the Little Woman's cooking was not truly great, but it wasn't quite that bad. So, I asked Ryan, "Why all the gymnastics?" He replied, "Satan is everywhere, and I must ward him off and rebuke him constantly. As for you, if you were smart, you would do the same."

After our first evening with our very own Messiah, I was amazed at his talents. He knew the Old and New Testaments; he was a first-degree black belt in karate; he could recite from memory the Constitution, Declaration of Independence and many other wonders. Daughter number two gazed admiringly, and I myself was dazzled by this soft-spoken holy spirit, for he was quite unassuming about all the talents he possessed.

After he left, she explained that since Burly Curly and Super Jock were going to be here to keep daughters number one and three company, she would need someone too. However, knowing our eastern lads, I knew there would be a great deal of friction with "our own Messiah".

He spent a few more dinners with us, going through the same ritual. He casually mentioned that he felt we had been touched by, or had encountered, a spirit that had given us a bad time. From the expression on daughter number two's face I immediately knew that she had told him nothing of our prior experiences. We were all amazed again at his acute perception. He went on to explain that once you have experienced this, you carry this oppression with you always. He also felt the tension among us, and said he would pray for us at his place of worship, to rid us of our lovely spirit. I said "Go right ahead!" A believer in spirits I was not one year ago, maybe—but now I certainly sang a different tune!

The day had come for Super Jock to sprout wings and head west. The girls were excited and planned to meet his Capitol flight at nine pm at LAX. Daughter number three was ready to go at four-thirty p.m., for she did not want to be late. By six p.m. the fog was so dense around our house that the TV man announced that LAX was closed.

I immediately jumped to the phone to call Capitol's Toll Free number, which I knew by heart, to monitor the flight. They told me they would land at Ontario Airport at ten-fifteen p.m. and bus the passengers to LAX for our pick-up. From the way that voice was talking, I knew from experience that it was lying. I called for another progress report at nine-thirty. I wasn't going to let daughters number one, two, and three walk in this soup, much less drive in it. They would land in Las Vegas at eleven-thirty and be bussed to LAX for our pick-up. The next call for a progress report, during daughter number three's almost convulsive state, "They will land at Ontario at eleven-fifteen and be bussed to LAX for pick-up, no kidding" Capitol's lady said. And I made her say "honest!"

The fog appeared to be lifting a little and off went daughter's number one, two, and three, for I couldn't hold daughter number three back with a backhoe at this point. I armed them with my nightstick and a baseball bat. I knew LAX after midnight, and told them that if anyone so much as looked their way to whack first and ask questions later. They insisted that I not go to witness the reunion.

Anxiety ticked on the clock as I awaited their call, for when they had arrived. Midnight. Then one a.m.—one-fifteen and the phone rang. It was not a female voice. Super Jock told us he was in Oakland and would be staying the evening, and he would fly out at ten a.m. for LAX. He was going to sleep in the terminal so he wouldn't miss the flight. I said "OK" and hung up the phone. Now daughter number one's voice was on the phone stating there was no flights and that Super Jock was in Oakland. I told her to get home as fast and as safely as they could. Daughter number three decided that they should sleep in LAX. There was no sense in making two trips. "SLEEP IN LAX!" I screamed. I would rather have them sleeping in the Bowery in New York City. I commanded them to get home, and get home now. They finally conceded and returned home at four a.m. PST. Daughter number three who just six hours before looked like a cover girl, now looked tired, windswept and dejected

Morning came, and so did Super Jock. From the looks of him, he was beat. I asked him if he had called his mother, and he said he hadn't. I ordered him to call her that minute to let her know he had arrived safely and still in one piece. He reluctantly did so. His conversation: "Mom? Yeah, I'm okay, yeah, I will. Goodbye." Now, I ask you how could someone like this run up a monstrous phone bill the way he did? Remembering back twenty years, I guess talking to your mother wasn't that much fun after all.

Daughter number three was beaming at her bleary-eyed beau, and Little Woman was taking over the mother role, commanding him to eat, get a shower and get some sleep. But Super Jock, beat as he was did nothing but eat and look adoringly at daughter number three.

Super Jock was followed shortly by Burly Curly in the first week in January, also on Capitol Super Sky Saver JFK to LAX. This brightened everyone's spirits, including mine. Now I knew how our troops must feel on foreign soil when the packages come from home, I never thought I would want to see these two again, much less be happy about it.

Now they have met, and as predicted, "our Little Messiah" and Super Jock disliked each other immediately, with Super Jock the more immediate. Super Jock verbalized that he, Messiah, "gives me the creeps" and "our own Messiah" with his discipline is trying his patience. Super Jock confided to me that he wanted to really find out if he was indeed a first-level black belt. I replied that I believed him and advised Super Jock to leave well enough alone, because I didn't want to ship pieces of him back to his family. After much talking, he finally saw the wisdom of my words and backed off to the arms of daughter number three.

Number one daughter was out of college for Christmas break and trying to convince Burly Curly over the phone that she had not been running around with every guy in Southern California. He would not believe this, and the phone meter kept running. "Poor Burly Curly" everyone agreed.

The Little Woman had perked up with Super Jock's arrival and really got into the Christmas spirit. Burly Curly would arrive on January fourth, 1982, and the Little Woman was getting happier about that. Signs from home! I only hoped she would still be happy when they left.

Christmas Eve, 1981, was not so bad. When Christmas day dawned we had a houseful. We had daughters number one, two and three; Super Jock and number one son, who was killing batteries with his football, basketball, and baseball games; "our Messiah", the Little Woman and me; plus a twenty lb. turkey which quickly became a five lb. blob of bones. All this made for a noisy and very enjoyable day.

Super Jock started verbally jabbing the "Messiah" and I felt he was going to get his neck broken, so I whispered to him, "Back off". I didn't want to witness a killing. He backed off for a while, but started right up again after the "Messiah" had learned to play every new game in the house better than anyone else, including Super Jock's claim to fame, the card game, "Uno". Now Super Jock is a rough kid, but he was in a different ballpark with this boy. He knew it, I think, for he backed off to daughter number three's arms and more billing and cooing.

Having seen strange faces appear in our yard, Irving Eureen appeared with, believe it or not, Laker's tickets. This was too good to be true. I hate basketball; I would rather stick needles in my eyes than watch one moment of a game. I passed these tickets on to Super Jock, who was happy as hell. In addition to being an All-State linebacker, he was also a good basketball player, many games of which he was now missing to be with us—with his near-fatal disease again.

Irving was inventing something to stop eyeglasses from coming off in sporting events-a wrap-around strap. I said that I thought this had already been invented and he exclaimed; "No kidding?" Oh well back to the drawing board" and left. I looked confused as I usually did when he was leaving. As he departed he said "nice yard. You know, if you get tired of your gardener, I have a lawn mower I'll sell it to you cheap." I thanked him kindly. The wife dropped the coffee pot as he left from sheer aggravation and we had to purchase another.

We heard that Dr. Fred's wife had delivered another male, this one named Marvin. If he follows in his brother's footsteps, I'm sure Dr. Fred will be doctoring twenty-four hours a day, just for his own sanity. We traveled to see the little tyke since we hadn't been to Dr. Fred's house for some time. We found it barely recognizable. Marin and Manuel had almost destroyed this lovely, two year-old home. The walls were five different colors; the wall-to wall holes, and the handpicked furniture which must have cost as much as our two cars, was in shreds and splinters. Dr. Fred's spouse complained to the Little Woman but she could not hear a word the Little Woman told her, because Martin was screaming like a banshee in her ear. She told a story of how she had gone to the supermarket and somehow forgot Martin and left without him, she then drove to her hairdresser (her hair was growing in again). She then remembered him when she was in curlers and being permed. She ran in her curlers, to the market to get Martin. He was quite pissed off, and called her stupid. Not too bad for a lad of six. I roared with laughter and sat and watched the circus for the next two hours while the Little Woman and Dr. Fred's spouse carried on with other mis-adventures.

I was winding up a week in the Midwest and flying out of Denver when I met a talking out of the side of the mouth gentleman, about sixty and we became friends. He lived in East Los Angeles and was right out of Damon Runyon. Even the name he gave me, Flip Turf, was exotic.

It seemed Flip traveled the U.S. patronizing every racetrack from Santa Anita to Roosevelt Raceway. Now, one vice I have never had is "the ponies" and I wouldn't even know how to bet on one. Flip, on the flight back, had familiarized me with "parley's", "Mudders," and all the jargon of the track. He allowed that in the last race he had bet on he had lost his silk flowered shirt, for he needed a flashlight to find his horse in the race, and had almost got his "melon" busted when he ran into some undesirables at the track. He was unique in speech and manner, and I loved him. I brought him home, but the Little Woman was not impressed with his necklace of turquoise and diamonds. I could see however that everyone liked his colorful approach to life. I drove him to his "pad" in East Los Angeles and departed, exchanging phone numbers but feeling, for sure, I would never hear from him again.

I was wrong. One day the phone rang and it was Flip explaining that he would like me to come down to his "pad" because he had something I might be interested in. Off I went. I knocked on his Spanish-style door. With smiling glazed eyes Flip and his "live-in" Hicky, welcomed me. He introduced us, and Hicky removed her blindfold that she uses when she sleeps. Then I noticed a thick, blue, acrid-smelling cloud. Marijuana. Flip was very high, feeling no pain, and Hicky retreated to the other room. Flip offered me a toke "pure Colombian" he said. I declined. I hadn't used any stimulant for quite some time, and I was not about to start then.

After the pleasantries were over, Flip took me to an off-room in his "pad" about the size of Kansas, and told me "Now, on to this stuff I happened, I need some bread to feed the ponies next week. I'm tapped out. Choose what you need for a nominal fee". I looked at something that could only be compared to a Sears showroom. There were stereos,. Fur coats, turquoise jewelry, shirts, pants, sweaters crewneck and v-neck, in assorted colors. Everywhere I looked there was more and more and more. It seemed according to Flip that many of his customers had placed their orders too late for Christmas, and now he was overloaded with his hot-boosted merchandise.

He brought out the topper. Three gross of Playtex girdles. He felt these would be a great snatch for me. I explained that the Little Woman is five foot three and weighs 115lbs, soaking wet, and I didn't think the need would be too great for a gross of girdles. I spied pantyhose, and I knew the females in my house used these like chewing gum, so I inquired. He stated "Fifty pair for a double sawbuck" and that's as far as he went, for pantyhose were his best-moving item. My greed was showing, so I took twenty-five pair for a saw.

I was amazed at the tales related to me by Flip. Some I cannot tell here, but the most intriguing was about his life in Philly in the late sixties. He and his brother Todd seemed to have stumbled onto a young man who today is a very popular mind reader and magician. Flip confided that this mental giant needed backing and an agent. He told me that a magician's act is nothing more than mind over matter, for in no way can he see into the future. Flip stated that "I didn't believe him, and conjured up the possibilities in my head of predicting sporting events, horse races, and many other good parleys," Flip went on. He continued, "They were booking him some small spots in juice joints in the east, making some bread, when I conceived the idea of taking him to the cabin belonging to a friend of mine. This was against my brother's wishes because he was working on a big deal to book the guy on a TV show and anticipated some heavy sugar from the venture. Against the Magicians wishes, I dragged him to the mountains to meditate in this cabin. I left all the racing forms for him to predict the outcomes. He pleaded that he wasn't able to. I left him there for a week, but he busted out on me, never to be seen again by my brother, or by me, but reappear he did, on several major talk shows. His career was very well launched, and wanting nothing more to do with Flip or his brother.

Brother was so pissed off he ran Flip out of town on a rail, and old Flip wound up in LA, there he stayed. His brother even put out a "hit" on him, according to Flip, because the Magician had made a fortune that should have been all his brother's until Flip had come up with the cabin-in-the-sky-stunt. He passed this off to experience

I knew then that I was in the major leagues with Flip, and I didn't want to get involved, not even one more inch. I told him to keep the sawbuck and returned the pantyhose. The last view I had of Flip, as I was leaving, was of him taking a long hard draw on his Mary Jane, while Aretha Franklin was blaring on his boosted stereo. As Flip and Hickey were trying to hear the foul words that Aretha blared out "Knock on your door and tap on your windowpane". I beat a hasty retreat and immediately had our phone number changed and unlisted. It wasn't that I didn't like him, I did, but I was playing for the Toledo Mud Hens and certainly he was playing with the Los Angeles Dodgers. I know when I'm out classed.

I still had Flip on my mind as we were going to LAX to pick up Burly Curly, and I watched him eyeing me nervously as I approached. You will recall that I had tossed him out on his ass just six and a half months before. He was slightly scared of what I might do or say. I relieved his anxiety by saying "Let bygones be bygones." We went off to our new home where Super Jock and daughter number three were still cuddling on the sofa. Super Jock and Burly Curly were glad to see each other, and Super Jock immediately told him scary tales about "our Messiah" and his spiritual stories. Burly Curly being very superstitious was scared of him from the start, and he hadn't even met him. I told Super Jock to knock it off, and he did.

We were a family again, with Burly Curly and daughter number one; Super Jock and daughter number three; our little "Messiah" and daughter number two; the Little Woman, number one son and me. Our weekly grocery bill was $152 and climbing, but I didn't care. Everyone seemed happy.

The New Year dawned a little brighter, and I was getting the old feeling of a family together again, when I noticed that Super Jock was becoming extra nice to me. He wanted to ask me something important, but didn't quite know how. Finally I cornered him and asked, "What is on your mind, my boy?" Mustering up enough courage, which must have been hard as hell to do, he stammered through a flurry of words, the gist of which was a request that daughter number three finish her school year out with her friends, and of course, with him back east. Now daughter number three averred that she hated California so much that she had really tried to adjust, but couldn't. If I would do this for her, she would be in my debt forever. I growled "I don't want you in my debt forever" with the sinking feeling that it would be best for her mental health to do this.

However, the Little Woman would also have to agree. We needed to sit down and discuss this, not only with the Little Woman, but also with Super Jock's Ma and Pa. Super Jock swore that they had already given their blessing; it would be cheaper to keep daughter number three, for she could not possibly eat up $158 dollars a month! That is what their last phone bill had been.

It was one of those cases where love for offspring will win out, no matter how much personal pain it might cause the Little Woman and me. This, of course was the beginning of the end of my life in the sun. The sacrifice was made for her happiness. We arranged for her to return east on February second 1982.

To her and Super Jock's disappointment she was not flying back with him on the seventeenth. I told them to knock it off, for the Little Woman was crying at the mere thought of her youngest daughter leaving for the east. I explained that if they wanted this to come to pass, they had better stop trying to have their cake and eat it too. Daughter number three is very bright and she agreed not to bug her Mom.

The Little Woman announced that come June eighteenth, when daughters number one and two and number one son are out of school for the year, they would be going back to sanity, with or without me. Daughter number three's trip was the straw that broke the camel's back.

Daughter number three left the "Land of Sun and Fun" on Capitol Super Sky Saver to JFK and to the already arrived Super Jock's open arms. With her went our parental hearts, and we were very sad. However, daughter number three was happy, and that was all that really counted, I was finding out.

The weeks dragged into March. With daughter number three, Super Jock and Burly Curly gone, the situation at home was again desperate and failing.

I had to go off on another junket, this one through the South winding up in Tampa, Florida over a weekend. Knowing that Spring Training was upon us, and Tampa being the home of the New York Yankees, I decided to take in a game that the Yankee's were playing. The Cincinnati Reds were their formidable foes. At all the games I had caught at Angeles Stadium in Anaheim and Jack Murphy Stadium in San Diego, I had noticed one thing: the dignified, non-screaming fan was omnipresent. This was a very cultured-type fan that I never got used to. I missed the screaming boo-birds of Philadelphia who, on a fine December afternoon eight years before, booed Santa Claus at half-time, because their beloved Eagles, at that time were not only losing the football game but were making asses out of themselves by just showing up. I missed the delightful New York fan that would think nothing of openly cursing a Tony Kubek or a Marv Throneberry, for all their 25,000 or so peers to hear and join in.

I was seated one day, watching the game in the warm sun and feeling blue. Most of the people watching the game were retired men of distinction and were a little more expressive and vocal than the well bred Californian, but not by much. It was the fifth inning and I was ready to leave because the sun was really bearing down on me, when a voice was heard screaming over the crowd, as Ron Guidry was pitching. "Put him in the book Ron. Put him in the book!" I recognized this voice for what it was—it could only be a bona fide Yankee, "kill the umpire" fan. "Put him in the book, Ron!" he screamed over and over. I was delighted and turned around to see a middle thirtyish man, dressed to the teeth in a softball uniform. Instantly I loved him. I was sitting over the Yankee dugout and enjoying the Bronx Bomber. Seven rows back he was still screaming and trying unsuccessfully to make a move on the Yankee dugout. He not only loved the Yankees, but by his moves, that they were his life and breath. I was tired of this game, but I loved him. The game was going into the twelfth inning and he was screaming as Lou Pinella was batting with two on and two out. "Sweet Lou", he screamed. "Do it to it! DO it to it!" Lou didn't do it to it and fouled out. I left. As I was going out the ramp I felt a tap on my sunburned shoulders and saw this fully outfitted Bronx Bomber wearing number fourteen. He was screaming, "Please can I have your ticket stub? I have to get Lou Pinella's autograph cause we wear da same number. Please, please, please!" He was almost on one knee now. He explained that the ticket man wouldn't let him near my seat without a stub.

Now anyone who has this much ingenuity and persistence cannot be rebuked, not at least by this now homesick fan, for the east fan. I handed over the stub, and I feared that he was going to kiss me. All he did was gruffly scream, for he was now very hoarse, "Thank you! Yu are do greatest, da greatest! Me and Sweet Lou have da same number and I'm gonna get him to sign my uniform," and away he sprinted. I don't know if he ever got that autograph but he certainly deserved to. I got into my rented Cutlass thinking "Now! There is a fan!" I whiled away the rest of the weekend reading "An American Death."

Business was finished Monday evening, so I booked an eastern flight to Atlanta and then to LAX. I was home by midnight but before I fell into a deep sleep I heard the Little Woman quietly sobbing in her sleep.

There was a sales meeting coming up in Reno, and I felt that a trip for the Little Woman would be in order. My production was at an optimum, and experience had taught me that there was no better time to ask for a favor than when you are riding a wave. My supervisor agreed to pick up the Little Woman's tab—plane, motel, car and food. She was somewhat happy and her spirits brightened. She said she thought this might help her recover from daughter number three's departure.

We flew out of John Wayne Airport to arrive in a very windy and cold Reno. I had five days of sales meeting, and she was free to roam Reno and shop, one of her favorite pastimes. We went to show after show and to a whirlwind of activities and dazzling arenas. She was almost happy. Possibly this would snap her out of her doldrums. I went from casino to casino telling her that I had to play a little blackjack every now and then. She scowled, for the Little Woman did not drop nickel one into those slots. Departure time arrived, and I could see that going back to our Golden Land was depressing her with every tick of the casino clock. I also had some bad news she wasn't quite aware of yet. I had lost all the cash we came with. She hadn't noticed because there was no need for cash; we signed for everything on the company.

I had fifteen cents left. I had to tell her now, hoping she had some cash. I felt sure she was tapped out and she was. She screamed, "What are we going to do for money?" The kids were coming to pick us up at Ontario Airport, and I didn't have fifty cents to get us out of the parking lot. I told her to call them to bring money. She, being a very proud lady, was not going to ask her offspring for their money. She was not speaking to me now. I felt this was going to be the longest hour on an airplane in my life. I spied a friend from the company who was flying back on the same flight. I asked Wess to please sit between us on the ride home and act as a buffer for her aggravation. West agreed, "Anything for you" and played his role perfectly. He had the Little Woman's spirits a bit brightened in the terminal and on the plane.

We landed at a smoggy Ontario to squinting offspring. I took number one son aside and asked him to bail me out of the parking lot. Luckily he did, with seventy –five cents. It was a silent ride home. I had taken a seemingly thrilling experience for her and turned it into a mess. She was now totally depressed and crying again because I had lost all the cash we took with us. Entering the car, we drove to the fifty-seven-freeway south; needless to say it was a very quiet ride. We were screaming at each other again for the next several weeks.

The situation at home was not at all humorous anymore. I knew now this was the end...finish...finito of our stay in the Land of Golden Opportunity. I didn't think either of us would live a free life outside a padded cell if we were not out of here pronto.

Go East Young Man

I had made the decision to go home because I could not stand the sorrow that this ridiculous move had caused. The Little Woman was better after the decision. Now, to try and undo everything that had been done. It would be tough because Reaganomics had put a damper on the financial aspirations of everyone in the east. This is the way it was March tenth 1982.

I called Wisconsin to squirm out of our lease. I feared for the Little Woman's sanity and mine. The move would have to be made immediately. I could get out of the lease and use my security deposit as one month's rent, paid till May first. I had to sell everything off that we had acquired in the not so golden Land of Opportunity because we still had a houseful of furniture sitting in a warehouse back east (on which you will remember I had been making payments these many months).

"Woe is me!" But love for my family is greater than any opportunity in the world, and I began the long, drawn-out process of reversing everything I had already reversed nineteen months earlier. I finally found someone who would buy the $2400 worth of sticks that eagle eye Chester had sold me, and I was very grateful for that. Daughters one and two had gotten an extra load of schoolwork so they could finish school early, as did only son. They didn't mind— just so they could get out of California as soon as possible.

The Little Woman peddled off the refrigerator and we were soon packing boxes again. Number one son, who had never moved before, was now on his third move in nineteen months. He couldn't quite figure out what the hell was going on. I overheard daughter number one remark to him "Welcome to the land of your father", as she called all the nonsense she had put up with in her formative years, when Dad was an active alcoholic. She was kinder now that it had been ten years since Daddy had touched the grape or the hop. She remembered being thrown out of many houses for her drunken father's non-payment of mortgage. The phone ringing with the enraged recipient of one of my spongy checks; the lost jobs and the drunken stupors; and the incident we all laugh about now. One day while her mother was cooking dinner on our $400 electric stove, earlier in the day needing a drink I had sold the stove to two drunken buddies for fifty dollars. They arrived with a truck and a scrawled receipt from me stating that they now owned the stove. They lifted it right out from under the Little Woman's peas and potatoes.

You always hurt the ones you love. Now I was doing it stone, cold sober. I was overwhelmed by guilt and remorse. I had really meant this to be a solid opportunity for all concerned, but I had screwed up again. I continued my efforts to make life somewhat bearable. I would do anything not to hurt this lovely group again, God willing. We were still unsettled in our decision in moving back to the great northeast. As I mentioned before, though, nothing beats a 3000 mile move for free meals and niceties. The situation was reversed, and the friends we had made in bimbo-land were taking us to dinner and giving going-away parties for us while I was in the process of resigning my position. There was the dinner at the Benihana in Anaheim one night; brisket at Ronald and Yuri's home; Yankee pot roast at Irene's (she was a good friend of the Little Woman; and I might add, one of the prettiest ladies of Spanish descent that I have ever laid eyes on). There was sushi in Glendora; and a lovely going-away party for the Little Woman at the unit where she worked. She shed a tear after that one for it was nice.

I called the movers and scheduled them for April twenty-first 1982. Boxes, boxes, and more boxes were being packed. Number one son's fish were down to twelve. They had continued to jump out of the aquarium at the rate of one per week. Naturally, number one son wanted to take the fish back on the three thousand mile drive. Daughter number two convinced him that he should donate the fish to his sixth grade class. Finally, he relented. His teacher was very happy and pleased with his gift, but he was still very sad about it. He truly adored my son and stated that he was the best student he had had in twenty-two years of teaching the little darlings.

Daughter number one and the Little Woman were so well thought of at their places of employment that their immediate supervisors vowed that they would never be able to replace them at the unit or JCPenny's. Daughter number two's teachers exclaimed that they had never seen a brighter, more well adjusted eighteen year old in their life. My employer responded by saying, "Who do you know that can take your place?" "Probably anyone" my man said. I walked out for the last time amid low-spoken well wishes and half-hearted attempts to be nice to me. I have one feather in my cap; all the while I was employed there Punk Goofball tried, but could never maneuver anyone or anything to get me fired.

The movers came on the twenty-first, right on the dot and the Main Man told me that since he had a very prominent, well-known person's belongings to move east, I was lucky because what was left of my furniture would arrive in only four days. You see, prominent person was moving 15,000 pounds of stuff east and wanted it there by the twenty-first. Since prominent person was moving only seventy miles away from us, my belongings would arrive on the twenty-fifth. "The twenty-fifth!" I screamed. "We're not leaving until the twenty-eighth! I had figured from the move west that it would take at least three weeks to move it 300 miles". He said "No way!" Every day he was late, prominent person was knocking $250 off the bill, right out of his pocket. Come hell or high water, that furniture would be there, because he had another prominent person moving from east to west, and that same situation applied. So my belongings whether I liked it or not would be there the twenty-fifth.

"Now where do you want me to take it Pal?" The address I had given him before no longer applied. I had to make a fast shuffle. The Little Woman called her mother and asked if it might be stored in her garage. Mother-in law reluctantly agreed. Thank God that was settled! Mover loaded and moved off my belongings along with prominent person's. I wired mother-in-law money so the mover could deliver the belongings to her reluctant garage. Now it was an empty house again. D-Day III, not until the twenty-eighth, one week away.

We were still being invited out for free dinners and goodbyes. It bears repeating that you can't beat a 3000 mile move east to west or west to east for free meal's. We needed them badly now. Free I mean.

The Little Woman was starting to sound like the Little Woman again. As we were passing through a store, I jokingly stated that when we got back east she would probably win a free trip to Hollywood. She just looked at me and said "I would kill them!" I believe she would too from her icy stare.

We were back to sleeping on the floor again. The realtor, Tammy Sunshine arrived to check over our rented property to report to Wisconsin whether we had been bad or good. It didn't matter. The $450 cleaning fee that Mrs. Renter had collected in advance would never be returned whether the house was as clean as a surgical operating room or looked like a shithouse. Tammy agreed in her fake, long gone from central Texas accent, that the home was "Positively immaculate." With the way things had gone so far, I was hoping Mrs. Renter didn't charge me anything or send me a bill for some unknown disaster.

The Little Woman's prospect for the refrigerator appeared to take the monster. Take the monster they did, and paid in cold, hard cash. We now had four days left and no refrigerator. Daughter number one had an unfinished project at college, and it would take her about three days to write the thesis. So we were left on the floor with no refrigerator. Tammy Sunshine not trusting us said she would be back on the day we were to leave to inspect the place again. She wanted to cover her little, wiggly ass as much as possible.

We were eating out morning, noon and night. The free meals had stopped. I visited Dr. Fred to bid our adieus. I really respect this man. He was one of the few good people, he and my Korean motel proprietor. He stated with much sorrow and embarrassment that he was truly sorry it hadn't worked out. I said I was grateful for all his help and that it was not his fault. He had done everything that he could have done. NO one could have changed the circumstances that had occurred. We parted, shaking hands. I noticed a little tear in the corner of his eye as I bode him farewell.

Two days before D-Day III number one son came down with tonsillitis. Dr Fred in his usual manner, prescribed and fixed number one son up and told me to have him take the medicine for ten days. When we departed I had a large tear stuck in my eye. I shall always miss this fine man and fine doctor.

Daughter number one was feverishly working to finish her thesis. I had to get my old secretary to type it for her as our typewriter was on its way east ahead of us (or perhaps even resting in my mother-in-laws reluctant garage by now).

The Little Woman needed her opal ring tightened. Our daughters had given her the ring on her birthday, and she would not risk losing the loosened stone. We went off to a jeweler in the Brea Mall who had been recommended by a friend. The jeweler looked it over and began working diligently with one of those little glasses scrunched into one eye. He had finished and I was about to pay him when I spotted two helicopters overhead with a beam of light swaying back and forth through the parking lot. I also saw three or four men, or boys, running. By now police cars were abounding and people were starting to notice what was going on. Number one son was away from us playing Pac-Man somewhere. It finally dawned on me that this was going to be a manhunt, and possible a shootout. Here I am again, right in the middle of an event!

"Holy hell! Where is number one son!" The cool Little Woman was getting excited, and I was having visions of shells screaming around us and a gunfight of the proportions of the St. Valentine's Day Massacre. The parking lot was now mobbed with CHIPS and bad guys. One bad guy was running toward us in the jewelry store when, from out of nowhere, two California's finest put as fine a tackle on him as I've ever seen, and had him cuffed and in the black and white before I knew what was going on. My hat's off to these two whoever and wherever they are!

It seemed there were two more bad guys left and they were jumping over cars and rolling. I didn't' see any weapons in the bad guys camp, but I hoped that number one son was enraptured long enough with Pac-Man or Donkey-Kong that he didn't decide to make a move now. Finally, the bad guys were cornered, roped and tied and whisked away with sirens screaming. People were wandering around thankful that it was over.

I found number one son who hadn't even known anything was wrong. "Let's go" I said. We headed for the bronze sedan, which had carried us, 3000 miles west; 25,000 miles around the freeways; and now hopefully would carry us 3000 miles east to sanity tomorrow. I noticed a footprint on the trunk of the bronze sedan. One of the desperadoes must have used the packed sedan as a springboard in his unsuccessful leap to freedom. Shaken, we left for home, to spend our last night in the Land of Golden Opportunity. That footprint went with us.

Morning dawned on D-Day III cloudless and smog less. A fine farewell to the band of anxious Westerners going east. Tammy Sunshine appeared and drawled, "Positively immaculate."

"We aren't getting the damn money back anyway, so knock off the bullshit Tammy" I thought and handed over the keys. She locked us out, and we piled into our respective cars. Daughters number one and two and the great white rabbit got into the blue hatchback. The Little Woman, number one son and I moved into the bronze sedan. I said it was only fitting that we should stop at Sambo's for breakfast before leaving and stop to fill 'er up now at one dollar one cent per gallon. The little blue hatchback was planted in the rear view mirror once again. I saw the great white rabbit looking stoically. We were off. But the Little Woman was not smiling. I asked, "why not?" She very carefully explained that she would when we had crossed the California line into Nevada, and not before.

We were all seated in Sambo's talking about how much we missed daughter number three and how anxious we were to see her again. We ate our breakfast smiling, paid our bill and departed. We headed for the friendly Mobil station to fill up. We self-served ourselves at those little islands. The little blue hatchback was empty save for the great white rabbit. Daughter number one was pumping the pink gold, and daughter number two was buying Coke and Dr. Pepper from the vending machine for the trip across Death Valley. Number one son was buying candy bars; he feared starving going across the desert. The Little Woman watched as I quenched the gulping thirst of the bronze sedan.

The sky was cloudless and the day warm. I thought of how perfect California weather really is. Number one son returned with his booty and settled into the back seat. The bronze sedan's thirst was almost satiated for the rubber guard, which had always been a pain in the neck to me had kicked to let me know it was satisfied. Daughter number two took 'her place beside the great white rabbit. I hoped that the cardboard, temporary Pennsylvania license would last the six more days I needed to travel across North America again. It was barely holding together after nineteen months.

I paid the gasoline man. But Southern California had one more small disaster to deal us. Daughter number one's strap on her stuffed tote bag broke and all of those nineteen year olds personal items were strewn about the self-serve island. We all went to help her refill her bag. Daughter number one and two were rummaging for lipsticks and mascara; number one son was picking up change and small packets of Kleenex; the Little Woman was collecting suntan lotion and neatly-wrapped small gifts for Burly Curly, while I was picking up perfume bottles that had not broken. The flurry had subsided, but macadam, saying nothing. After a short time, she was still staring down, so we all converged on her. To our utter disbelief we saw, on the macadam, staring back at us all, a lone diamond earring!

The New Beginning

Originally I had intended my tale of woe to end with the reappearance of the lone diamond earring. Events followed, however, that so defied belief that had to be told.

Our trip east was uneventful save for a few minor skirmishes. The overheating of the little blue hatchback and the wearing out of a few tires, hardly compared with what had gone before. A bit more disturbing was number one son's obsession with characters and creatures with names like Donkey Kong and Pac-Man. With his behavior bordering on compulsive, I had to physically yank him from game rooms in Kansas City, St. Louis, and Louisville, Kentucky.

We were now homeless vagabonds hoping that mother would take us in, without too many "I told you so's". We saw our first signs of the east in Kansas City, Snow! Good ole slippery, white, cold snow. Daughters number one and two and number one son frolicked in it to their hearts content. Once again I found myself shoveling snow from the bronze sedan and little blue hatchback with my Holiday Inn Travel Guide. Again, I slipped and cursed but this time no injury. "Must be a good omen" I muttered to myself.

As we made our way farther east I saw the glaze in the Little Woman's eyes begin to disappear. On we go St. Louis, Ill. and Indiana. I· began to think about that expired cardboard temporary license plate on the bronze sedan. Now, the Keystone State is not quite as liberal as the Golden State, so I re-routed the caravan to barely touch Pennsylvania on the homeward trek. We traveled south of Louisville, and Lexington, Kentucky into West Virginia north to Frederick, Maryland; east through Baltimore; northeast to Wilmington, Delaware; north to Trenton, New Jersey and north to mother's place in eastern New Jersey, not touching the Keystone State at all. They would surely have slapped my ass in jail driving on a two-year expired cardboard plate that was a bit weather-beaten to say the least. We were home!

Mother was happy; daughter number three was there to greet us with Super Jock by her side still glaring at me. Now these two lovelies and number one son became very "Western" in the "Eastern" atmosphere. Each statement they uttered was followed by "fer shur" or "gag me with a spoon". Number one son was talking like the world traveler, and it was becoming very obvious now, that Sister Alice had migrated for the homecoming, to verify that Dear Old Dad had just absolutely dragged the family from their Paradise in Eden.

I walked out and said a prayer. I had good reason to pray. I had returned to mother's place with (a). no home; (b). no prospects of a home; (c). no job, (d). no prospects of a job. The Little Woman was stating vehemently just how much she had hated everything from the desert to the snowcapped mountains of the Golden State. It was becoming redundant, so I suggested, "Why not just tape the conversation, rather than repeating it? Then it will be handy for any and all to hear." She replied "I would if our tape recorder weren't in storage!" This was a sly allusion to the nasty Certified letters we had been receiving from Storage Man concerning the selling of our worldlies, if I didn't come up with some hard cash soon. This maneuver to get us all on track would have to be one of my best if we were to endure and be a family again.

Life was passing quickly with me trying to stay out of mother's and She-hound's way. Whoever remarked that too many cooks spoil the broth was very correct. Ever more correct in the case of the Little Woman who has been known to have a bad time just boiling water. I can recall a time early in our marriage when my Bride made a three-layer cake just three-quarters of an inch high. I won't go into detail about our bouts with stomach cramps and nausea stemming from some of her other culinary attempts. Mother, on the other hand, was a master at all the delicacies I love. Through experience I had learned that trying to use mother as a tutor for the Little Woman at the range was to no avail. Mother's instructions always went "A little of this, a little of that." She never really shared her time-proven secrets because no one really knew what "a little bit of this, a little bit of that" were.

Daughters one, two, and three were really putting on the California dog for all their old companions telling, in depth, all of the exploits and adventures they had encountered in the Land of Plenty. Daughter number one was leading the way with her stories, mostly bullshit. Hmmm. The apple doesn't fall far from the tree, does it?

The Little Woman was in a delicate condition known as "I want my furniture. I want it now!" As you remember my original plate was still on the bronze sedan. Of course I was also still holding the Certificate of Origin on the car, which had never been registered. The local lending institution wanted their Title, and they wanted it now. The Moving Man was threatening again, and I was having no luck house hunting. (A newly renovated farmhouse sounded great until I found that "newly renovated" meant they had changed the paneling from turquoise to red.) with no job yet, money is again at a premium.

I decided to tackle the most immediate problem first. I had trouble deciding which was more important: to keep the car (the lending institution has said they will repossess it if a Title is not in their hands in fifteen days); or to keep my worldlies (the Moving Man wants ten percent in fifteen days or the mementos will go to Sheriff's sale). I concluded these two items were of equal importance so I had to attack both at once. The Little Woman, number one son, and I journeyed to Moving Man's warehouse to be greeted by ole "Call me Tom." He appears glad to see us, and can't wait to deliver the proverbial "I told you so". He also felt bad that my belongings were trapped in his vault. The only key that will open it is money. I tried "Open Sesame" to no avail. From my point of view, what's good for

Ali Baba is certainly good enough for me. The Little Woman remarked that one of my major problems is just that-believing the books I read.

The Little Woman wanted to peek at our life, entrapped in the wooden crates. "No dice!" Call-me-Tom states. "Too much trouble." Obviously, since our furniture has been here from November 1980, to June 1982 it is packed in and packed in solid. Since no citizen in his right mind would dodge a Moving Man for almost two years and deprive his family of their belongings, call-me Tom wants to hear one word, see one color; money and green. The Little Woman takes ten percent of our storage charge and gives it to Head Mover, Brian. He swooped in at the sight of the green, scribbled a receipt and said, "We never really want to sell anyone's furniture" and handed number one son a miniature replica of one of their famous red, white and blue moving vans, complete down to the company logo and windshield wipers. That made number one son happy. I promised "I'll call you in a month". I was trying to be as positive-sounding as I could, and I hoped he didn't detect the fright in my voice as I had absolutely no idea how the hell I'm going to get him any more money in the thirty days our receipt states. Remember, securing employment was not one of the two most immediate problems. Number one son is learning life the hard way from the mistakes of a fantasy-ridden father who is coming down to earth FAST! His comment was, "We'll never see my bunk beds again". I assured him that he would. After all, what other father would buy his son a truck for $180—that's what the Little Woman had just handed over to Mr. Mover.

The next stop was the New Jersey Board of Motor Vehicle Registration to pay the sales tax and get the bronze sedan titled. We waited in line to be allowed to finally pay the State of New Jersey $196 in exchange for a title which the Little Woman Express-mailed to the lending institution before the ink was dry. The ceremony of taking off the cardboard plate to replace it with the cream and blue steel "Garden State" license was brief. We returned to mothers for celebrating in the kitchen.

It was there and then that I decided to write this book. Everyone laughed, except the Little Woman. It made me feel good to think she still believed I was literate. I started with the title. I have now felt a presence that had attached to my situation, what form it was I didn't know, but he or she or what ever it was, was very ominous.

With two major problems temporarily taken care of, I pursued job and housing. The Little Woman read the papers religiously for housing. Once again we were traipsing through old, new and neutral homes that are all the same: dirty, small and over-priced. "Reaganomics" is widening and has put a damper on my search for sustenance. At last I am getting over the three hour "jet-lag" and feeling and looking better again. The score, though is still: no housing, no prospect of housing, no job; no prospects of a job.

I began to call old acquaintances in my search for employment to get the repeated response, "Gee how was California? Gee why did you ever come back here? Gee are you crazy?" "I sure as hell must be, I'm talking to you" kept running through my mind. "I WANT AND NEED A JOB" I scream. "Any other conversation is NOT NECESSARY." I realized that I was talking a lot like our realtor friend, Sherman Nearsworth. I begin to understand how he got that way. He must have moved east and then moved west again.

Mother and the Little Woman are getting along as expected with two women and three daughters under the same roof. Sister Alice began glaring and subtly inquiring if we had seen the house on Bullman Street. If it were the Kresge Mansion I don't think I would live in it, if it happened to be on a street named Bullman. I walked out and prayed some more. It worked.

The phone rang. It was an old friend from my prior company. He needed a straight-commission representative for the Philadelphia area. He asked "are you interested?" I replied "Very much so!" I agreed to meet him at eight p.m. Sunday in Philadelphia to discuss it. This is to be a straight commission deal. That means: no salary, no expenses, no sell, and no eats. But I had to get something. Here I was spending money just as quickly as though our income was adequate, but our income was actually non-existent! Until Sunday, I would continue dodging mother, Sister Alice and Brother Lester who are glaring and asking if I have seen the house for rent on Bullman Street. Their manner is starting to appear as it was ten years ago, as I was just getting sober, after a month on the drunk farm. Losing everything, as my life was dictated by alcohol, up to that point. After losing house, car, many jobs and all respect from anyone, I am still trying to keep a family together. I the great one wound up on welfare, after my fantasy world was destroyed. Having to move in with my Mother and Father to keep us off the streets.

It did not sit well with everyone, that there brother/son, was a drunk. They must have had a flash back as to days gone by.

I was rolling along pretty well on my book fantasy. First and foremost: the revenue from the book. Then of course the notoriety and guest appearances on the Johnny Carson Show. You'd think I'd learn by now. Not this fella. With all the gold I receive from my masterpiece I'm planning on visiting the Far East. And I'm not even keeping it a secret!

Burly Curly has appeared on the scene begging to be my ally. It seems the boys are traveling by night and sleeping by day. Super Jock and daughter number three are romancing again, but the romancing is curtailed by her job at a fast food steak house. Daughter number two is flashing big brown eyes at the algebra and trigonometry books, as she will not be sidetracked from her quest to be a nuclear physicist. Number one son has begun to miss his buddies in California and feels he is much too good for this part of the country now. The Little Woman is close to panic as our creditors have passed the pink letter stage and are now sending mailgrams at all hours, reminding me of my obligations. I have begun trying to make some money by hustling people to a certain used car lot for a small bird dog fee if they buy one of the "cream puffs".

The Arrival

Sunday comes. I must make plans to pick up "Buddy" at the Philadelphia airport. Ted has no peer when it comes to the technical end of industrial petrochemicals. His ability is surpassed only by the naiveté of his wife Lonnie. Lonnie has Ted in hock up to and over his Pierre Cardin turtleneck and he is sinking deeper by the hour. The drive to Philadelphia from mothers' is two hours. The flight is late of course. I have much to miss, as I reminisce in the Philadelphia airport, about my days and nights in other airports. The gypsy is not gone, and I know it never will be. I enjoy watching the jumbos land and the passengers files through the jet way to the open arms, or not so open arms of loved ones.

Ted appeared, smiling and shy, with his best Clark Kent look. I've always felt that at any moment Ted might run into a phone booth and reappear minutes later flying about, stomping for truth, justice and the American way. This has never happened, but I still wait. We exchange pleasantries, shake hands and head for the baggage areas.

Walking through the concourse Ted states he's in a world of shit with our former company and needs business. Since he always overrated my abilities, he feels I'm the boy who can save his life. I know from nothing about industrial products, except that they are blue. I tell Ted this. He scoffs and says it's easy and no problem. My mind does a replay of a sales meeting in Reno when he held seventy-five hard nosed distributors in awe of his explanation and demonstration of polymers, nitrates, phenols, refraction circles and many more unknowns. Easy for you I thought, difficult for me. We grab the luggage and head for the bronze sedan. I help Ted carry and pull. "What are you carrying in here?" I asked. "information and materials to make you a success" he replied. It will take a helluva lot more than that to do the trick! He scoffs in his own shy style and insists, he will pound what has taken him fifteen years to learn into my thick skull in just four days.

As we headed North on I-ninety-five, he stated that everyone at the home office was out to get him (I am glad he hasn't lose his paranoia) to Lonnie who just maneuvered Ted into a white Corvette that he can't afford Since she just finished maneuvering Ted from Virginia Ave. to Park Place and didn't pass Go. He bitched away the whole two-hour drive and I felt hopelessly sorry for him because I knew what was coming. In the glare of the oncoming headlights, I noticed a tear forming. He finally admitted that Lonnie had confessed to some misdeeds. These errors I want to know nothing about. It must have been very fresh in his mind since he is reacting now. He sobbed openly "what am I going to do, she is my life my everything. I am going to kill myself." Holy Hell! I think. "He's not here for anything but hand-holding and comfort. This problem has moved to a higher plane than I can handle. I don't need this, I don't need this. The pressure of my own doings have been squeezing me so that I can't take four deep breaths in a row without passing out, and now I am expected to play nursemaid to Clark Kent!

He settled down to short chokes and wheezing, and I tried to be positive. I said things like, "it will work it self out. It'll be over soon". I knew full well that Ted, being too busy with his development of a better hydrogen bomb, somewhat neglected his marriage. We arrived at his motel and he checked in. He didn't want me to leave, but in my unstable state, I couldn't handle anymore of this. I hoped my Father Flanagan image had been put out to pasture, but the collar must still show. I begged off since tomorrow would be a long day. Since I had much to learn in the world of fatty esters, I should get a good nights sleep. He conceded as we shook hands and I turned to go.

In the dim light of the motel hallway, he looked more like Clark Kent than ever. I crawled into bed that night intending to catch up on some of my own marital homework. But number one Son had again settled into our bed to sleep with mommy and daddy. I said nothing to the Little Woman, of Clark and Lonnie's dilemma.

Upon arriving at Ted's room the next morning, I knocked and there was a delay. I could hear his voice on the phone. It was only seven-thirty a.m. and I wondered whom he could be talking to. Room Service, I thought and waited. He came to the door, looking like he hadn't slept at all, and he was in the same clothes and the bed wasn't disturbed. He was back on the phone in a minute. From the tone of his voice and his expression, there is trouble in River City!

At seven-thirty am here, given the time difference of three hours, by my calculation, he has Lonnie on the phone at four-thirty a.m. It didn't sound too promising as a string of "I forgive you's" came from Ted's trembling lips. I waited through more pleading…eighty-thirty…eight-forty-five. Finally, Ted kitchey-cooed and turtle doved his way to bidding Lonnie an endearing goodbye with the promise that he would call every hour on the hour to make sure that she was home only with their roguish mutt "PLATO'.

We went off to breakfast and I ate through a stream of tear-jerking, "Why me's" and "She is my whole life". He was talking about tapping the phone when he returned. I mentioned that it might not be such a good idea. Number one, it is illegal. Number two, he might hear something that his head wants to hear, but his heart doesn't. So, I warned, "If you do this, be prepared for the very worst." But Technical Ted is a stubborn man and I was sure that he would tap the phone anyhow. By this time its eleven am and we have accomplished zilch in the way of making me a successful industrial coolant salesman.

I started to push for knowledge from Technical Ted, but I was wasting my time. Making me successful was the very last thing on his mind. He's back to the phone again reciting his fourteen digit credit card number which I memorize and would be using shortly. (Sorry Ma Bell, but survival is survival, and I'm taking it where I can get it by now) Eventually I was to use this card many times over the next six months, saving mucho dollars on my telephone bill. Ted's conversation went on. Now it is twelve-fifteen, and still no knowledge from Ted. "Just hold on" he ends his conversation. Back to his room to learn.

Ted's red message light is blinking on his turquoise phone. He calls the desk and the message is read back. A blank look appears on his very blank face. I knew better than to ask, but he told me anyway. It seems his Superior at National Company in the far-off Land of Plenty wanted him to fly back immediately and meet with him as soon as possible. We both knew that this could mean one thing and only one thing—termination. Up till now I thought I had troubles, but I was finding out that I didn't even know how to spell the word.

Ted was back on the phone again, making flight reservations from Philadelphia to LA. He secured a six pm flight and we were off to Philadelphia Airport, midst double moaning. He feels Lonnie will surely blow out all of their plastic now that she feels threatened, now that the job is probably gone. He was a totally shattered and forlorn man.

We arrived in Philadelphia in plenty of time, and off Clark flew. I had wished him well, and he had apologized. He stated that his Sales Manager, in the east, will take call me. He promised to see that the details of my appointment as a rep would be followed through, by a fellow named John Lookingood. He assured me that John would contact me soon. I headed back to New Jersey.

Upon my arrival, the Little Woman advised me that she had seen a new townhouse development in the paper that was being built in Bethlehem, PA. I told her nothing about the new development with Ted, but said we would go to Bethlehem the next day as Ted had been called back to the West Coast to solve some emergency.

It seems that the rent on these townhouses starts at $500 a month. "I don't have it, but I'll get it" I thought, "though I don't have the slightest idea how." Then out of the blue the idea struck me, "The book! This book! I'll sell shares." Far out, you think? Well you are right it didn't work. P.T. Barnum said there was one born every minute, but I could not find any, no matter how hard I looked.

The homes wouldn't be finished and ready for occupancy until August thirtieth. That meant we would have to grit it out at mothers for one more month, amidst the stares and pained looks from everyone, and even the she-hound's dismay.

Beauty Is
Only Skin Deep?

The phone rang at our unfurnished new townhouse. One the other end was "John Lookingood ." He stated that he and his new boss, Rob, would be in Philadelphia the next day to meet with me to discuss my appointment as a rep. I was to pick them up and not be tardy. I had no other choice at this point. Our move had been easy since there was nothing to move. All of our worldly goods were still safely in the Moving Man's vault.

I waited at Gate fourteen for US Air Flight 1141 and the arrival of "John Lookingood" and Rob. I had no idea what they looked like, so it was going to be fairly hard to identify these two with only the words of "Lookingood", stating that he would be the "Best looking human to get off the plane" and that Rob looked like "Big Bird from Sesame Street". Then I spied two that fit. "Lookingood" was just that—the most beautiful human I had ever laid eyes on—impeccably dressed, gold chains swinging from his wrists, diamonds adorning his tanned fingers, shoes polished to a blinding sheen, hair styled and not a one out of place. His eyes were direct green and he flashed a set of beautiful teeth. Now, I'm not a bi-sexual person, but if I were, "John Lookingood" would be the guy to go for. He was beautiful! But, oh God, was he errant! I learned this after just five minutes of his looking to see who was watching him and hearing his third statement that Ted had told him that my Old Lady was good looking. He wanted to know if this was true. I ignored the question, but he didn't notice, because he was busy trying to catch his reflection in anything that would reflect his handsome image! Oy, veh! He primped constantly, straightening his tie, running his hand smoothly over his brown tresses.

Meanwhile the new Sales Manager, Rob, was insisting that I become a distributor and order $15,000 of product. I replied, "I certainly will, providing you give me six months to pay". He quickly answered "No problem". Now I knew from this statement that with "Lookingood's" actions and Rob's confidence I had here two real beauts. They were both trying to make passes at anything female. "Lookingood" was getting plenty of positive responses and Rob seemed content with the overflow.

We collected baggage, got them settled in a large Philadelphia hotel, and sat down to a meeting. "Lookingood" checked the mirror and excused himself. His suit was wrinkled so he would shower and change suits. Rob entered from the adjoining room in his Christian Dior robe and nothing else. This was the scene at a would be business meeting with two executives from a Large National Company. Lookingood was evidently out of the shower because the hair dryer was humming. Dinner was the next important item on the agenda, they argued. The French food that Rob wanted was too far, so they decided to "go Italian". That is what Lookingood decided. He had the credit cards and the boss didn't (Rob is Mormon and Mormons aren't allowed credit cards)? Rob had relinquished grudgingly but thank God, I was pretty hungry myself. I wanted and needed this free meal. Still, nothing was settled about my position for "Lookingood" was wondering if he should wear the beige or the blue serge tomorrow. I wished I had problems like that. The night wore on, and I wore out after eating and wanted to go home. Nothing had yet been accomplished about my future.

They were to fly from Philadelphia to Baltimore in the morning. They told me they would contact me soon. I did learn something that day, though: the more stripes a necktie has in the lining the more it costs. So, no day is ever wasted.

I drove off into the night wondering if I had enough gas to get home and also, what the hell it is all about.

I did have enough gas to get home, but as to the other question I still haven't the faintest idea and don't think I ever will.

Surprisingly enough, product comes to my house in the form of "free". Lookingood came through! The letter from Rob stated that there was about $750 worth and I could sell it and keep the money, I was going to do that anyway, but is always nice to have permission. Within one week I received my representative's contract, all neatly signed and stating that for whatever I sold I would get twenty per cent commission payable no later than the fifteenth of each month. At last! Light at the end of the tunnel! God is certainly alive and He listens!

The Little Woman was sounding like a broken record, wanting her worldlies again. I didn't have the money. I had been paying for the necessities of life and nothing more. More threatening letters from the boys at the collection agencies. Ah, life can be beautiful! I was working very hard to keep life and limb together while Daughter number one griped constantly about not having money for school. Daughter number two seems to be taking it all in stride, and Daughter number three had become distant and foreign number one Son was happy because there was a stream nearby, and a stream means fish (what is it with the fish?) Thank God, at least for now dollars are appearing and we can eat.

Sad to say Daughter number one had given Burly Curly the gate and that made for sad times for Burly Curly would not go down easy. He and I almost came to blows because he blamed me for breaking them up. This wasn't true. With all my problems I couldn't have cared if her beau had been Jack the Ripper. The only thing I was trying to do then was survive, and that was absolutely all I could handle! As for those that don't know what I mean I can only envy and feel sorry for you at the same time. These experiences do build character if you don't die trying to build your character. As for me I would really rather not know what this is that I'm talking about.

He Must Have Gotten Up on the Wrong Side of the Bed

It was now September twenty-fifth, 1982, and we have as a unit, been sleeping on the floor for four months. Believe me it doesn't do anything for posture, but at least there is no wrong side of the bed to get up from. The Moving Man had not been paid for four months and was reacting accordingly. His most recent letter says:

Moving Man
Allentown, PA

Dear Mr. Barna,
After numerous attempts to reconcile your indebtness with us, I am notifying you of I.C.C. regulation 646, which states that unless full payment is received by October first, 1982, your household goods and possessions will be sold at Public Auction on October tenth,1982. As it would be to your benefit to satisfy this indebtness immediately. Any questions do not hesitate to call.

I remain Sincerely Yours,
Mr. Mover

Now, how is that for scaring the hell out of you? No ifs, and or buts—if the money isn't in his hands by October first, 1982, I lose our life. What this letter did to our family relationship is beyond description. Daughters numbers one, two, and three's longtime dolls are going; number one's son's Tonka trucks are going, all of our movie film of the kids growing going. Christmas, Easter and birthdays are going; not to mention things like TV's, dining sets and beds—all going. The Little Woman was beside herself, and I was rapidly getting there, too. I immediately called the ICC and asked if such a dastardly deed could be done. The sweet voice on the other end assured me that it could, indeed, be done and advised me to beg, borrow or steal the money. I chose number two. I had a friend whom, ten years before, I had taken under my wing when he was a starry-eyed summa cum laude graduate entering the automobile business and the real world for the first time. I called Jed and stated my problem, and asked if he had any banking contacts. Since he was now the finance manager at a large car dealership in the area he was my last ray of hope on a sinking sunset. I had no real employment to qualify for a loan of this size. Jed, as pleasant and humane as always said "I will certainly try". Try he did.

The next thing I knew I was sitting in front of the Loan Manager of a local lending institution, Mr. Roy Bent, answering a lot of questions about my hapless life, my puberty, and just why I needed the money. I was as polite and nice as I'd ever been, even though he wasn't. He said he would let me know the next day. A long eighteen hours ensued. The Little Woman was now snarling her words. The ever-present voice of my mother-in-law was sighing "I told you so" and "You could have married that nice, young Dr. Bruce. By the way he still asks about you. I saw him yesterday at the A&P". As always she was a real positive force in my situation. She has a knack for making a bad situation impossible.

I phoned Jed and asked him to call Mr. Bent to try and push him over the edge to make the loan. He agreed. He was back to me within five minutes saying "You want your furniture, Don't run—fly to the bank before he changes his simple mind!"

The dial tone had not yet faded away when I was in the lobby asking for Mr. Bent. I went into his inner sanctum to sign, and then off to the Moving Man with the money. The furniture and mementos were saved! We could have our possessions in four days. Our belongings had been trapped in his warehouse from November 1980, till now, October 1982. It will take him four days to get to them! Friday! A happier day there never was! It's amazing that the things you take for granted every day, just sitting, laying or standing in your home, can create such excitement, but it sure did! The Little Woman, however, never did really forgive Mr. Mover for losing her squeegee sponge and her Avon perfume boot. I sent him a Christmas card though. He didn't send me one. Imagine that! I was one of his longest customers, too!

It was a relief to have that problem out of the way, but the ink wasn't dry on the receipt when a letter arrived from the California bank to whom I had offered to pay the interest on the loan I owed them. They refused. Now, they were talking legal maneuvers and judgments. The only thing I owned was—yep—the newly re-acquired furniture. The Little Woman is not a dab happy about this one, nor am I. I've had it. "Truly" I thought, "there is no gravity, the earth sucks." I've had it. I called them. On Ted's credit card of course. I told Mr. DePlano that he could do whatever the hell he wanted because I'd had it up to my prominent nose, and he and his bank could go to hell. I used many other words that I later regretted saying. He stated that it was out of his hands and into the legal department. (They are still trying to collect, and I am still maneuvering. I don't know how it will work out. If it resolves before I finish the book, I'll let you know.)

Go West Again, Young Man

Thanksgiving, 1982 dawns as I was checking my funds. The tally sixty-two dollars and forty-seven cents in the checking account; twenty-one dollars in the savings account; four dollars and fifty cents in wrapped pennies; and the Little Woman has twenty-six dollars and twenty-six cents in mad money for a total of $154.17, about enough for groceries. I'm flat broke, destitute, busted.

As I pondered a way to create some cash, the phone rang. It was Clark Kent (alias technical Ted). He was happy to say his life was "straightening out" and asked how mine was. I replied "Don't ask!" He said "Not to worry" and told me he had gotten connected and explained to me how I could make a quick $2000.00—all legal. but he added I would have to go back to the land of plenty. I explained my very negative cash flow situation "I can't afford a trip around the block, much less 3000 miles to LA". "Not to worry. I'll make arrangements for you to be flown JFK to LAX as soon as possible. I'll be back to you in three days."

The Little Woman had overheard this conversation, her statement was simple and to the point, "you can go back to Sodom and Gomorrah, but leave me and the offspring out. No siree! No way!" End of statement. I told her we needed the money and must go; secretly I couldn't wait to get back to my haven, She said, "Go if you must but not I!"

I anxiously awaited Ted's promised phone call. The phone rang. Not Ted, but John Lookingood, calling to complicate my life further. After two of his best jokes, the first one being told is the best. It seems two Englishman are rowing down the Thames river, one fellow yells to a row boat passing by, ay buddy lend me one of your oars, the other fellow replies "these ain't oars, there me sisters". He then proceeded to make me an offer of a job with my former company he was not sure he could pull it off but he would let me know by December tenth. Good ol John Lookingood – and looking out for me. Bless him! He said he would call back! Just a week ago there was nothing, now there were two great offers. The Little Woman rasped, "don't get your hopes up". I detected she was growing very sour on this thing called life. Who could blame her, I was getting sour too. But I still acted positive—one of my best attributes I feel to this day. Because I have always felt that positive thought coupled with positive action can do wonders but sometimes it's so damned hard!

Ted called back and told me everything was set up the tickets would be waiting for me December sixth at JFK. As soon as I arrived in LA, I would meet with two fellows Roger Macaroon and Eddie Jablonski, who would advance $1000.00 of the $2000.00 of salary immediately on my arrival. I mentioned that I had no place to stay to which Ted responded," Well I can't do everything." He told me to get it together and he would pick me up at LAX on December sixth. "Don't be late!" You might well be asking yourself why the hell these two guys would do this for me and I'll tell you I guess, it's because I'm so damned cute.

The next problem was to find temporary living quarters in Sunnyland. Wow almost a repeat of 1980. I could think of only one guy who would take me in. That one guy was Ronald and his wife Lotus Blossum Yuri. I called and he states "Of course, Lizard Lips". I called Ted back "Great! See you in a week."

Lookingood called back too I told him about my planned trip to the west coast. I still wanted to leave the door open with my former employer. I really didn't know too much about this operation of

Ted's and there was no way the Little Woman would live in Southern California again. I gave him Ronald's phone number and told him to contact me after the sixth of December.

Once again I am 747 bound for LAX at eleven PM December sixth 1982. I had twenty-seven dollars in my pocket twenty dollars of which I had to borrow from Daughter number one.

I am welcomed to Ronald and Yuri's home for my stay in sunny California. With open arms, Ronald opens with a "Hello scumbag". I now know nothing has changed in our relationship. Yuri is as gentle as ever and just as beautiful. Ronald has been practicing his favorite sport – laying under a 1969 Camaro, and loving it. His handshake produces grease and grime, as I try not to notice. Clark Kent has departed for his love nest and states he will pick me up at nine a.m. for our attempt to sell coolants in San Diego. I notice a new addition to Ronald's family, a chunky muscular brown pit bull, named "Caesar".

Caesar has started to eye me with two marbles protruding from a block of granite known as his head. I back off. Ronald says, "Don't worry about him, Owl Breath" for he at worst would only love me to death. I don't buy it. Caesar is wagging his stump, I remember a dog wagging his tail or stump, in this case will not bite, so I amble to the couch and Ronald and I reminisce. Ronald's little girl just whacked Caesar with a greasy wrench and Caesar does not react, but looks at me like I did it. I can tell by looking at Caesar that he does not like me and is not even open for negotiation at this point.

Yuri makes a great Japanese dinner. I ask seconds, and get it. We talk some more and the time lag has caught me, so I announce that I am going to retire. Yuri has my room made up, unpack the Tourister, brush my teeth, turn the covers back and settle in for the night.

Ronald raps on the door, announces that it is six A.M. I drag my carcass from the bed. I walk around the corner of the ranch house to go to the bathroom and Caesar is guarding the door and his stump isn't wagging. I call for Ronald, he laughs, tells Caesar to leave. Caesar does and I am clean.

Clark Kent appears at nine a.m. and off we are on the San Diego

Freeway to peddle our wares. Clark is again lamenting his situation and now I have the distinct feeling that I am a sounding board as we spend the day trying to find a phone tap that is not only economical but also small as Clark is going to tap his home phone. I warn again that he may hear some things that he may not want to know and have recorded for posterity. He cannot be dissuaded. Radio Shack supplies his needs. Clarks mind is not on work for we are now heading north on the San Diego Freeway to my new California home and Clark states to call our friends who are financing this operation for my car and directions.

Clark bids me ado and gives me all the necessary materials to be successful. We shake hands and I mention that the phone tap among all of the other negative aspects is also illegal.

Caesar is wagging his stump at the door. He looks like he may be, just maybe accepting me. He lets me pass. I undress, change to my shorts and sneakers. I walk to the backyard, pick a dozen oranges, turn on the juicer, instant fresh orange juice. Yes, California does have some advantages, fresh juice, a balmy seventy-five degrees and skin that turns pink from the sun.

It is four P.M. P.S.T and I must call the Little Woman to find out how things are going, also to tell her that a check for $800 is on its way to her, for the necessities of life. The Little Woman answers, seems somewhat glad to hear from me but gladder to hear about the 800 scoots that are in transit, from Anaheim, to our waiting checkbook; Daughter number one gets on the phone and she starts asking questions about Southern California and I notice a longing for the sun in her voice. The Little Woman also mentions that Rob, the National sales manager called and wants me to call him in California at his office. I bid the Little Woman, Daughter number one, and number one Son a goodbye.

Rob has called for one of two reasons, to ask me to fix him up with a broad, or heaven forbid, they are going to hire me back. Here I am two miles from his office embarking on anew career and just getting used to the idea of same, and now complications.

I call the National Company, ask for Rob he announces that I am rehired as of January second, 1983. There are stipulations though, I must not even talk to Clark Kent much less be in his company, which I am. Rob thinks I am in Pennsylvania and here I am two miles from him just leaving Clark Kent. I do want this job for a number of reasons;

A paycheck.

A paycheck.

A steady paycheck.

So I am in a quandary. He states that all of the necessary papers are being typed and mailed to me and he expects me to be in Ft. Lauderdale, Florida January fifth, 1983. He is kicking off the New Year, at a very plush hotel on the beach, with a sales meeting. I slobber and grovel and thank him for his offer and accept. He states again to stay away from Clark or he personally will wring my skinny little neck himself or worse fire me! Oh yes, he adds I must move to Pittsburgh, Pennsylvania and that $1800 is allotted for my move (remember the eighteen hundred dollars). The money will be given to John Lookingood to dole out to me as needed, because Rob feels in my financial state, I would keep the money. Insulted I agree. Wow, two careers. Another move. I have to figure out a way to keep the $800 I just received and get out of California. I must also stay away from Clark Kent, not to mention to talk the Little Woman into moving 300 miles to Pittsburgh. I need to weasel out of my agreement with Roger and Ed, in less than one month.

Ronald comes home and I tell him of my situation, He snickers, shakes his head, says "You are real Scumbucket" and gives Caesar his leather belt to chew on and chew he does. Ronald laughs as the belt is shredded and Caesar is licking his chops, looking at me and making a low gurgling sound. I am hoping at this time that ol Caesar is not looking to take a piece of my skinny little neck, for there will not be much left of me after everyone gets through with it. I don't tempt fate and go to my room to think this through, as this is what the ol scumbag is up against;

I've already accepted money from Ed and Roger.

I have to be in Pennsylvania soon.

But I do have $190 in cash.

Rob cannot find out about my association with Clark or it's curtains before it starts.

I have to pay Ronald something for living there.

If I am honest with Ed and Roger and tell them I want out, there is a possibility of them stopping payment on the money that is on its way to the Little Woman.

If the above happens all the checks that the Little Woman writes on the check that will be returned and one of those returned checks will result in the repossessing of my car.

And last but not least the persuasion of the Little Woman to move to Pittsburgh Pennsylvania.

One mess after another and it all started with Dr. Fred's "You will not repent moving to the land of fun and sun". Do you believe this? Well there is but one thing to do, put it in God's hands, say a prayer, go to sleep and things might look a little better in the morning.

I awake, Caesar doesn't, his slumber allows me to go to the orange tree and pick ten more oranges for fresh juice. I do feel very healthy form all this juice. It's amazing how the mind can manipulate you into thinking that all things are great when they are anything but.

I call Roger and after about four tries reach him at the Rath Skellar. He seems to be on his way at eleven A.M. He tells me to relax and enjoy the sun for a couple of days, as he and Ed are going to buy the new car for me to use. God, I can't let them do this, can I? But I have to buy time for the check to travel four days, clear the bank, five days. That's nine days, which takes me to December seventeenth. My mind's made up, I am going to put on my most pathetic face tell them the truth, yes, that's what I'll do. Right after the check clears.

The Little Woman calls and says Rob has called again and wants me to call him. Call him I do and he states that the plane tickets and advance check have been cut, and are going to be mailed December fourteenth. Also things have changed, he obviously does not trust Lookingood either as he will give me the money for my move to Pittsburgh in Ft. Lauderdale on the fifth of January. I am too far into this, and I can't back out at this point, so I say OK. Oh yes, he adds again stay away from Clark because Clark is stealing business with his new venture. "Stay away from Clark!" he is twenty miles from me. How the hell can I do all of this? I can, I tell myself for survival is survival and as I mentioned before those of you who relate to this will know and those of you who don't, well you won't.

The Red Eye

It seems as per the Little Woman that a new twist has entered the old ball game, in all the past confusion I neglected to file 1981 Federal Income taxes and Uncle Sam has notified me of such. The Little Woman is not too happy and I think she smacks of temporary insanity. Again this added pressure on my return to the banks of the Delaware.

I call Ed to formulate a meeting. He agrees to meet me at the Rath Skellar, as I have no car, Ed states he has an old Volkswagen that will be at my disposal if I can get a ride from Ronald's to Bert's. What has happened to the new car, I wonder?

I wait for Ronald. He obliges by taking me to Fred's Union seventy-six station to pick up the old Volkswagen. Well old is not a descriptive word, it must have been at the beer hall Putsch in 1923 when a certain maniac was launching his career in "How to win friends and influence people". Beggars cannot be choosers. Fred hands me the keys and in a cloud of smoke I am off to the Rath Skellar to meet with Ed. Upon arriving at the Rath Skellar, I notice some very expensive autos parked outside, which is out of sync for this type of establishment.

Maneuvering to get all of this together will certainly take a man of high caliber and extreme cunningness all of which I am amply endowed (remember the old positive attitude). First I will have to meet with Ed.

I call on Eddie, reaching deep into my repertoire and to my amazement Ed is understanding or he is just sick of me. He tells me to sign this promissory note for the thousand he has advanced me and not to forget to include my address. He then tells me to get the hell out of his sight for he is getting pissed off. As calls keep interrupting our conversation, I ask to use his phone to call for a trip to LAX as I still have the return ducket for travel. Ed calls his regular gopher Juan (pronounced Guan) to take me to the airport for Bon Voyage, the sooner the better, I think. Juan fires up the rickety van with the chain link steering wheel and the orange pelican on the dash next to the Virgin Mary statue. Off we go on the Garden Grove Freeway when I announce to Juan that my belongings are still at Ronald and Yuri's house. Juan is timid and meek, but now as he states "Holy Chit, you dumb gringo, I got work to do I con be dribing you all ober de LA basin and if you want de airport we are going now or nebber". "OK Juan", I state just get ol' Willy to the airport and I won't bodder you anymore". I will call Ronald later for them to pack my clothes and ship them. This should make the "Ol' Scumbag" ecstatic as I am sure he has a few better things to do with his time than to pack up my belongings into a box, cart them to the Post Office, pay for them and ship them to me and hope that he gets reimbursed for the charges. Oh, I do bring joy into many lives now don't I? I call Ronald and it is done.

I leave the rickety van lickety split at LAX and go into the terminal of which my ticket is associated. There is a flight leaving in forty-five minutes to Newark, New Jersey via Baltimore. There is room and I am ticketed and seated, smoking aisle, please. Now I have to procure transportation from Newark. I call the Little Woman on Lookingood's credit card, as I have memorized his also. I state my case as briefly as possible, the Little Woman responds positively. The flight will arrive at eight A.M. EST. Since Newark is one and a half hours from my townhouse the Little Woman will have to leave at six A.M, she agrees and I wait. She is very personable, not biting at all. This amazes me. The check must have cleared.

I settle in the Jumbo, it roars, shakes and lifts above the ocean, turns and the no smoking sign blinks off. I settle back, it is twenty-three-fifty PST and I can now relax.

We are now bumping and grinding down for it is dawn and Baltimore is below me. It will be a half hour layover, you may deplane if you want to, but be back soon.

The jumbo rolls and roars, we are off for Newark. The time passes quickly and we bump and grind into the state of North Jersey and stop.

I sight the Little Woman perfectly coffed at eight a.m., snuggle and get into the car. I feel very relieved that I am out of Los Angeles in one whole piece. See I told you prayer works. Homeward bound, a shower, shave and a phone call from Ted asking me "What the hell is going on?" I tell him that it is called "ballis abstencious". An old Latin phrase meaning "NO BALLS". I want to go to work for the old company, back to the world of twice a month paydays, telephone credit cards and expenses. He seems to be disgusted and tries to apply guilt, but I will not allow it. I have had enough of the old adventurous nonsense. Goodbye, farewell and amen!

The plane tickets have arrived from Rob with a check for expenses. With Christmas one week away the expenses will not be necessarily business related. My employment is to commence officially January third, 1983. More literature in the form of insurance forms. Ah, it feels good to fill them out, as I had no form of medical coverage for almost ten months. Now try that for anxiety attacks at three in the morning. The good Lord prevailed and protected, as He will if He is allowed to.

Christmas comes and goes. It is a four on a scale of eleven. Children are somewhat content, but as late teenagers and early twenties go, they are concerned about themselves alone. As all of you parents of people about to be people will know!

By the Sea,
By the Sea,
By the Beautiful Sea

As the newly acquired plane tickets dictate that I am to fly to the National sales meeting in beautiful Ft. Lauderdale, Bahi Mar Hotel, January fifth 1983, via Atlanta. I swing and sway into Lauderdale at twelve-thirty PM, leaving the snow behind and into a gigantic windstorm, zoom bump, rock and grind to a halt to be met by none other than John Lookingood and looking good he is. For he arrived three days before to turn and tan. He has his white suit on to glorify his tan and teeth. He looks magnificent, and I have to remark that he does. John will play father to me for six days and nights. We retire to the top-level restaurant for a bite as Lookingood is looking for skirts or pants of the female persuasion. I scan the menu; the cheapest entrée is a hamburger for nine dollars and fifty cents. Wow, here I am going first class again. Lookingood insists on going for broke, because you look like you need it. I do and I do. We finish reminiscing; I haul my borrowed Tourister to the front desk to check in, as Ronald has not sent my belongings back yet. "Check in! Yes sir, room 714 Sir, yes Sir." Room cost $141.00 per night plus tax. Off to the elevator and into the room overlooking the Atlantic and the towels look great. It is now four PM, John mentions that he is going to freshen up and since the meeting tonight is at seven-thirty he really should get going.

I settle into my new domain to experience this newfound luxury. I call the Little Woman legitimately for the first time in one year on my own credit card and tell her to hold on because for the first time in a long time things are looking better, not good but better than they did for a long time.

I arrange my sparse wardrobe and put the free shampoo in my newly acquired free briefcase, that Lookingood graced me with. I have prepared to meet my newfound friends at a reception in the Swordfish Room at seven-thirty. The phone rings, it is Lookingood giving me instructions on how to act in the presence of royalty tonight. Royalty it certainly is, from jokers to jesters and back again.

I arrive at the Swordfish Room to the aroma of steak, rye, bourbon, shrimp, leather and scam. I am first introduced to the new V.P. of marketing Joe Baker. It seems his claim to fame is wrestling with live snakes and tries to kill them before they kill him. I dislike him and he dislikes me. Rob enters in splendor, barking orders and borrowing fifty dollars from Lookingood who digs for the money. Rob states to me "Good to see you again", against all odds he says, and he being who he was,"the greatest" has swung this job for me. I guess that means that I should be eternally grateful, I am and say so. Rob just says to eat, and eat I do, steak kabobs, large jumbo shrimp, teensy weensy shrimp, some funny looking gray things, it was great. Next, to meet more of the team, Floyd Forge and elderly man with a not so elderly lady on his arm and leg, and with his free arm jacking Jack Daniels into his elderly mouth! Next is Ted Kralik a new addition, likeable, short, blonde and sensible. Robert Tentman is next, elderly white hair portly and talkative. He likes me immediately and indicates this. Through discussions, I find he is twice as scared as I, and not as good at disguising it. He explains that Rob is looking for an excuse to get rid of him soon, since he had his gall bladder operation. He promptly shows me his scar. Lou Briskett is next. "Hi Ya kid, If I lying, I'm dying", I have met this one many times before

as a car salesman, he is the prototype, back slapping jokester, brown
nosing troublemaker, asking if I got the $1800 dollars for the move
yet. I answer no, not yet. I immediately see friction between Lou and
Rob, but I discount it. Into the Swordfish room strolls Bert and "call
me Charlie". Bert is different and Charlie will give Lookingood a run
in the beauty department. I see the inventive Rob has worked out a
promotion for the distributors called "steak em". Old Bert is the steak
promoter and Charlie is an employee who is involved, but I don't
know how. Bert begins by shifting very shifty eyes around to survey
his pawns, obviously liking what he sees. He looks into my shifty
eyes and there seems to be a bond instantly. Between myself, Bert
and "Call me Charlie" the evening passes with the announcement,
from Rob that all of the distributors' wives can expect roses with the
morning paper. I am astounded with all of the frivolity and frivolous
spending, this company sure has changed, but out of the corner of my
eye I see our "Big Guy" giving Rob a not so nice look upon his
announcement. As Rob is feeling the effects of the frivolous
spending, he doesn't pay any mind. I feel he should, but who am I,
Just a fellow trying to recover from near catastrophic events. The
evening ends with megabucks spent on this short four-hour tenure
with six more days and nights to go.

I arrive promptly in the Dolphin room for our first meeting at
eight AM. I am thankful, after perusing the Dolphin room and seeing
the puffed faces, shaking knees and bleary eyes. I am grateful that I
retired to my room and went to sleep early. . I am the only fresh face
in the lot, and the meeting begins. It goes on for four hours with no
breaks, one hour for lunch and four more grueling hours of listening
to great promises, great egos, and great bullshit. As the old saying
goes "the mind can absorb only what the seat of the pants can
endure". The seat of the pants was sorely tested in the nine-hour
marathon, in the room with the gold dolphin on the door.

The phone ringing jars me awake on the fourth day; it is Bert
stating that one of his friends from up in New York has just happened
by on his small boat. Asking if I care to join him and Charlie for a
small party aboard the old tub. Upon further conversation I decline,

only for the reason that after four days of more luxury than I should be allowed to have, I have a meeting with Rob and Mr. Baker. I am sure they will bust my balls with direction and regimentation in the morning. Bert seems to understand and bids ado. It seems I missed quite an extravaganza on the tub. Rodney Dangerfield, for he was making a movie in the area attended the get together and had all the boys in stitches for hours. Also the old tub turned out to be a one hundred ten foot yacht, I knew there was something I liked about Bert and Charlie.

I am beckoned by the yellow phone in my room again; Rob is on the other end. He instructs me to proceed to suite 463 to meet with Rob and the snake charmer for my meeting. "Oh, by the way" he states "don't mention the $1800 moving money. I smell something rotten at the Bahia Mar and think so. Rob says, "Hey pardner, I got you this far, I'll get you all the way". He has and he will with a few major detours along the way.

The meeting goes well with the snake charmer, telling me what they expect from me. Since it seems the goals given are unattainable, I state they can be met. I am getting the feeling I am here as an item. I can't put my finger on it but it seems I am Rob's pawn.

Don't worry pardner, it's okay pardner, give'em hell pardner. As we close the door on the snake charmer, Rob whispers I'll give you the moving money in March in Baltimore. Then you can move. I feel with this statement Rob has certainly spent the $1800 buckaroos and I am being set up. Now what do I do? I have some options; let's look at them;

Call our "big guy" and tell him what has happened.

Call the snake charmer and ditto.

Shut up and say nothing.

Play it by ear, knowing that Rob has spent the money and eventually will ask me to say I received it in Florida.

"A" and "B" are out, for our "big Guy" doesn't know me, and the snake charmer doesn't like me. It also appears that Rob has the old snake charmer in his pit.

So I opt for "C" and "D" trusting my gut feelings, as they have never let me down when I allowed them to work, with the assistance of a Supreme Being.

The last day of meetings is here. Rob starts off by introducing Bert, who will enlighten us on his brilliant "steak-em" promotion. Bert is introduced and moves magically through slides and graphs but the magic appears to be leaving Bert, as I notice he is sweating and becoming very pale, he appears not to know what he is talking about. He is stumbling and rumbling and heading for the door pronto. But he cannot move magically enough to get the door open for his exit, which is hurried. I am convulsed by laughter. I can't control it for now Bert is rapidly trying to get the hell out of the Dolphin room. Finally, with one last great tug and grunt Bert is free and on the other side of the giant dorsal fin door.

I have to excuse myself for I cannot stop laughing at the fact that no one except Charlie has appreciated Bert's performance makes it all the more hilarious. I find Bert shaking uncontrollably. He states, "That fuckin dolphin door was stuck like glue". I put my arm on Bert's shoulder trying to reassure him that no one really noted his exit, for they were all interested in the VCR tape that Rob was showing of the meeting so far. It was hilarious, but to appreciate it, one really had to be there, believe me.

God Grant Me the Serenity

The meetings close with Rob and John Lookingood being extremely buddy buddy. Floyd Forge with another young gal on the arm and still jacking Jack Daniels into his elderly mouth. Lou Brisket asking me if I heard the one about the China man, and relaying that I didn't, but I have a funny feeling I am going to. The snake charmer glaring at everyone, Bert thanking God it was over that he and Charlie pulled it off. Mr. Tentman, whom I've grown to like, is still showing his scar to anyone who will look at it. I am feeling lower than dolphin dung, for I can feel what the next two months will bring. I am sure that Rob would have hired The Prince of Darkness himself, for the opportunity to get his hands on 1800 unencumbered dollars to spend. How he managed to do this I still have not figured out.

I take a taxi from the hotel to the airport and catch a flight to Atlanta. By now the weather had turned extremely foul. The flight was rough, but manageable. We slid into Atlanta amidst hail and ice. Now hail and ice are no problem for airports that deal with it on a daily basis. Hail and ice are enough to close Atlanta airport and it did, just as we landed. No flights going out, none coming in. It is two-thirty P.M. I have the feeling I will be in Atlanta for sometime. I was. Staying in Hartsfield airport for roughly seventeen hours is not recommended, for anyone.

We left the next morning at seven-ten a.m. It also seems in the rush, that they forgot to put food on the plane. Since everyone on the plane was fat, they voted to go back for it. So, off the taxi and return to get breakfast for the chubby ones. I don't mean to be mean, but of all the passengers on board, all I had seen when the vote was counted were many flabby arms extended up to return to the gate, for the food. While a minority of skinny limbs were up to head on home, without the grub.

The Little Woman again is waiting at the airport to pick me up for the umpteenth time. Home we go. Daughter number one is proving to be very difficult, Daughter number two is coming around, and Daughter number three is up to her old ways with Super Jock now on the scene. Who is finding out that all of his High School heroics, now that he has been out of the womb for one year don't amount to much in the real world. He doesn't seem to be adjusting. Number one son has found a new bevy of friends, male and female. As time is taking its toll, for he is thirteen going on thirty-five.

A new covey of male birds have taken up residence in our midst. Tall ones, short ones, slim ones, fat ones, nice ones, not so nice ones, ones in cars, ones on motorcycles, ones walking, ones staggering. It is a strange covey for some stay long some fly quickly and some just seem to beg to stay. Daughter's number one, two, and three seem to have the situation in hand as the flock responds to snapped fingers and glaring looks. The birds are also as selfish as the hens they are courting. I must surely have forgotten what it was like at this age. As everyone is telling me they have the same problems and they remember what it is like. I am sorry, I don't.

Things seem to be going in a positive direction as the paycheck arrives bi-weekly. Establishing my credibility again slowly.

My Fun Gland Isn't Fun Anymore

For all of you ego driven macho males, I would warn you not to read this chapter as it will not do your masculinity any good. Believe me I know from whence I speak. Amidst my wonderful paycheck every two week world, I am feeling grand and also feeling like I am sitting on a walnut and my urine flow is not flowing, this Monday morning in the year of the Lord (whom I will be contacting many times in the next twenty-four hours) 1983.

I struggle through the morning bloating and dribbling, chilling and fevering. I tell the Little Women of my predicament of not getting rid of my water, she states sensibly to go the emergency room. I say "nah" I will fix this myself with mind over matter and a lot of water. Dumber things I have thought but not for a while. The morning extended to the afternoon and so does my bladder and belly, which is now, rock hard.

One week before I was involved in a "not my fault traffic accident" being clobbered at a stop sign by a new BMW with a BOY TOY inscribed license plate, by a slight fellow with a very bad attitude blaming me (as I was not moving) for stopping at an intersection that no one and I mean no one stops at as he points with a limp finger to me.

As I am writhing, waiting for the insurance adjuster who is

scheduled for two p.m. to see my vehicle and adjust. The fever and pain is starting to rule and now there is not even a dribble or a drab of water exiting my body. More water (stupid) more advice from my wife (go to the emergency room, smart) more mind over matter (stupid) no dribbles (painful) fever escalating (wavy). I will beat this thing. "I don't need no stinking emergency room" Sequence of events:

A. Adjuster adjusts two-thirty P.M.

B. Do not feel like arguing with Adjuster.

C. Adjuster leaves, water and pain do not.

I now can not find a comfortable position at all lying, sitting, crouching, angling, walking, spreading, non-spreading, all to no avail. I've now had about eight hours of this and still trying to mind over matter it. For even I know what awaits at the emergency room. Since my water is not coming out by itself someone or something will have to take it out by artificial means and none of these can be any good.

Eleven hours of this and I finally relent that obviously my mind does not matter, as my thoughts now are very distorted and wavy. As I finally have enough courage to see just what temperature my body has heated to 102.4, reads the old mercury, oral thermometer. In the distance I hear the Little Women Waverly say emergency room or when————ready————go——me——. I am now hearing about every other word.

I now succumb to calling Sally, who is a very capable nurse, and close friend who lives near by. I relate my tale of woe and ask what is the worse thing that can happen. She asks, "When is the last time the old urinary tract was working"? "I relate that it was last night about ten p.m." Silence," What? What is the matter with you are you crazy, do you have a death wish"? All kinds of questions that as I am hearing every other word went like this;

Sally; What————crazy

Me; uh huh

Sally;——you——a——wish?

Me; oh

Sally; ——worse thing——happen is—urine—will back——
the kidneys———blood——will occur.

Me; (since I am not understanding nor hearing well) I pass the
phone to the Little Women who by her expression, I now know that
I am in a bit of trouble .My aversion to doctors and hospitals are from
experiencing treatment and care of my mother and father's illness.
Which was a comedy of errors. But not so funny for us that watched,
plus compounded by the behavior of the amigos, who carried the title
of doctors in my previous chapters, but not the same ones.

Things are really getting distorted and wavy. As now I must go for
help, as the bottom line of the Little Woman's conversation with
Sally is that

A. Urine will back up into the kidneys.
B. This will kind of put a kink in my body.
C. A blood infection will occur.
D. This is not healthy.
E. They can fix it.
F. If it is left too long they (the Amigos) can't fix it.
G. I die.
H. The pain and fever has now escalated to the point that I am
Numb.

The Little Woman states: "That when you decide to get this taken
care of, wake her up as she is going to bed". I call emergency care.
They give me directions, but I am hearing every third word now. I
gingerly walk to my truck, traverse the I'm not sure directions

And every bump, ridge, pebble in the road is indescribable pain,
that rhymes with rain that it is doing now. In my distorted sojourn I
sojourn to the wrong one, as this one is closed. I now have seven
miles back home in a manual shift, hard riding truck. It is truly A
Turn For Worse.

I shake the Little Woman, she is up and we are now sojourning to
the emergency ward at our local hospital, which should have been
done eight hours ago, as it is now twelve-thirty a.m.

I creep into the emergency room and a Fifty-Something Nurse

greets me with "may I see your insurance card". Not, what is your problem, nor, how are you doing? Insurance card, please, because nothing and I mean nothing happens until that card is produced. My wife provides it and something happens. I am given a sheet of paper with questions about my condition. It now appears that the pain is so great that I doubt that I know my own name, much less the mind-boggling questions.

Questionnaire:
Name_____
Address_____
Town_____
State_____
Zip_____
The nature of your condition_____

Nature of my condition, nature of my condition! Hah I can answer this one "I CAN'T PISS."

I state that to the Fifty-Something Nurse and I also exclaimed to her that if she can fix the nature of my condition. I will give her a thousand dollars. Now, she doesn't bat an eye and says, "If I wait one more hour you will give me fifteen hundred dollars". Even in the nature of my condition I find this hilarious and like this Gal. She was correct, right on the money, for I would have given everything materially that I own, to correct the nature of this condition.

I wait and suffer and suffer and wait, finally Mr. Barna, will you waddle this way. I waddle that way to be greeted by a forty something female doctor who asks of course "What is the nature of your problem?" Also a sixty something nurse enters. I am now much more delicate in my reply for now as I lay on the gurney they are very much in control and in no uncertain terms let me know this. "I can't seem to urinate and I feel a lump now becoming like a baseball in my scrotum" I meekly reply." Flip over on your side "states Miss Doctor. She is now putting a rubber glove on and quicker than you can say prostatitis, her rubber-gloved finger is up my ass, picking and probing, much to my dismay. As I, being brought up thinking that women are meant to be loved and idolized by the male species. Now this very pretty female doctor with her finger up my ass for now what seems to be an eternity. I wouldn't stick my finger up any bodies ass for no, and I mean no amount of money or notoriety that would come my way Miss Doc, states very sharply, "That this procedure is necessary for proper diagnosis", and I mention, why I don't know, "that she has very nice teeth".

Sixty Something Nurse is still lurking and writing. For Miss Doctor is finally making her move towards me. Doc's finger is out of my ass. On your back, sixty something nurse is sticking needles in my arm, finds a vein and in the same motion grabs my once flowering manhood, which is now not even a bud. She states, "Awe, look at that little thing". Now for all of macho male America, I have a message for you. We ain't very macho laying on a gurney. Catheter coming, more females starting to gather around, around this mere shell of what was me. Sixty something, with rubber tube in her hand states, "that if the prostate is really swollen and the catheter will not go by this happy gland", they meaning her and Mrs. Doctor, will have to aspirate the urine out of my bladder. I, very weakly ask," How"? She produces a very large needle that obviously will go into my bladder, via my belly. Believe me fellas, there are no atheists in foxholes and none on a gurney. Needle in arm, eyeing the bevy of females that have gathered to watch this, (I assume students of something), watching a sixty something nurse armed with catheter in the right hand, Miss Doctor with a very large needle pointing to my very naked belly and all that is there.

I am prepared for worse, as even I can see that this situation will get a lot worse before it gets better. Sixty Something Nurse grabs my manhood with ease and authority as she has done this before many times, in the well-lit cold room. In the state of mind I possess, my manhood responds to this by trying to hide from her, perky little penis is not so perky anymore and shrinks making it difficult for sixty something nurse to insert the catheter. Mrs. Doc stated, "That if more than 210 cc's of urine exit, I will be staying tonight". No, absolutely not, I don't care if 600 cc's are emitted, I am not staying here tonight and state this to all within earshot to hear. I notice a glance from the Little Woman that tells me that I really have no choice in this matter. She is shaking her head, as if to say, there he goes, trying to control the situation, when he can't even control his body functions.

Catheter ready, Sixty Something Nurse has a two fingered strangle hold on my manhood, ready, set, go. The initial jolt cannot be described except to liken it to a fireworks display going off in my head, blue and red stars pummel my brain for what seems to be decades. Something is moving in me to get something out of me amidst this glorious display. I hear faintly that the catheterization is successful and that little tube has gotten by my happy gland.

Oh, happy times, no aspirating the bladder, but I still have a way to go, as my water is filling up the plastic bag to the tune of 160cc's, immediately. The flow slows, 170 cc's, 185 cc's and starts to dribble to 190-194-196, and stops at 196 cc's. Fourteen cc's short of my exile. Mrs. Doc states that I am staying for observation. I state with more strength than I really thought I could muster," That I can kill myself as well as the hospital can". I am going home now as you (the hospital staff) have accomplished what I wanted you to do. "Thank you and have a nice life as I am leaving". There seems to be a high level conference of sorts with the Little Woman and I can tell that she is telling them that her husband goofy as he is will leave, even if he has to crawl on all fours, leave this hospital tonight. The bevy of students, Mrs. Doc and Sixty Something Nurse are looking at her with a look that can be described as, better you than me, being married to HIM!

Catheter disconnected and anti-biotic in my arm disconnected and my brain starting to connect, as things are less than wavy, as the mainline anti-biotic is probably kicking in. Common sense is starting to creep in and I think maybe I should stay, as it is now about four a.m. I am very weak now, but a flash of sanity takes me back to 1979 when my father was lying in a room similar to this, screaming in pain and anxiety, with no one attending him. I go searching in a panic, for the "do no harm oath taking doctors', but I can find no one available, with the exception of a doctor and nurse exiting one of the empty rooms. He was zipping up his fly and she looking very satisfied and disheveled asking, "who is screaming"? Not even sounding remotely interested in my fathers suddenly horrid world. All that I can think at this point is two balls for the Doc and three strikes for my dad and he is out. If that is not enough, another thought comes galloping back to Dr. Creole, who unbeknown to me, as I go to him to have a cyst removed from my neck, only to find out later that allegedly murdered Mrs. Creole the night before. Needless to say his mind wasn't quite on removing a cyst from my skinny little neck. The cyst has appeared a few times since his unsuccessful try and his uttering, "That we shall pray that it is not caansoooor", as he rolled his words in his home grown dialect.

The prognosis agreed upon by the medicos is prostatitis, a neat little chronic problem. My mind is clearer and I understand chronic means, I am going to have this problem for a while. "What can I do I plea"?

The pretty little lady Doctor explains that after a certain age, (mine) the prostate is a sitting duck for infections. It must be flushed constantly and water is a very good flusher. I probably drank a total of forty glasses of water in my whole life to this point. But if this will help, I am now resigned to being a bottle of water carrier; like the ones that I chuckled at and maligned in my manful way. I now carry this lovely strange liquid with me constantly. It seems to be doing the trick. It takes a while to get used to it, but then every time I think, this is nuts, (drink water, run to bathroom, drink water, run to the bathroom etc.) I think back in order:

(1) Sitting on a walnut
(2) Can't walk
(3) Gurney
(4) Catheter.

There are many things in life that are swell to repeat, sex, smelling roses, eating chocolate, playing and watching baseball, even maybe raising teenage girls. But a catheter in a male is definitely not one of these. One catheter and one swollen prostate will suffice for a lifetime and hopefully for eternity. Thinking of all this my mind snaps right back to snapping the cap off another bottle of water.

On one bright March morning, I am stumbling from my bed, nursing my prostate, turning on the coffee and grabbing the morning paper, I read. My head is getting clear from the brown liquid, when the headline on page six C reads; LOCAL MAN CHARGED. My brain explodes as I read; the local man has the same name as me to the letter. Since no age is given I read on;

It seems he has enticed an eight year-old boy and a ten year-old boy into SEX ACTS with him. I can't believe it. There is my name. No age given and no residence. What a feeling it is, indescribable, shame, guilt, total confusion. Hate for the old namesake disbelief and fear. I run to the bedroom to show it to the Little Woman. She groggily awakes and reads. There it is again, William R. Barna me arrested for moral charges. Barna this and Barna that mentioned ten times in the article. Why couldn't this guy have been a murderer? A burglar even a guy who kicks old ladies in the ass but not this, sodomy with eight and ten year old boys, and other illicit sex acts. This truly almost destroyed what was left of my head.

After much thinking and talking and calling the newspaper to print that, this is not the same guy who is me. The newspaper was very understanding and empathetic by noting just that, that "that guy", was not "this guy" who is me. The feeling still exists to this day even though that guy is doing seven to ten, for his crime. I hope he never gets out or if he does, he moves west.

They say for every adversity there is a seed of greater benefit. Surprisingly enough, the greater benefit from this was my wife, daughters, son and friends; all told me that of all the crazy things I have done, this would never be one of them. In all of their minds this would be the very last thing that I was capable of doing. It was unanimous, no greater feeling than that. Save one Joe Pastor a friend who winked and said you can tell me the truth Willy. But, that was what I expected him to say and it was taken in the vein it was intended. With that I asked Joes' boy of eleven, if he wanted a piece of candy. Heh, Heh, Heh…

Finally getting the old noggin and prostate semi-straightened out from those two nearly fatal blows. I travel throughout the east, my new territory. Then on one fine April morning at the Holiday Inn in Belle Vernon, Pa. my green phone rings it is the Little Woman. I am astounded to hear the Little Woman's voice telling me that the snake charmer has called and left a message for me to call him ASAP, concerning moving money. Which at this time has not been received, and I am betting that it won't be,

I wait until the office in California is opened for there is a three hour lag, I call. Mr. Baker, please.

Voice: "Who is calling?"

Me: "Bill Barna"

Voice: "Just a moment"

Snake Charmer: "Hello Bill, how are you?"

Me: "Fine, how are you?"

Snake Charmer: "Bill, just a few questions concerning your moving expenses."

Me: "O.K. shoot."

Snake Charmer: "Did Rob give you any money in Florida?"

Me: "Nope."

Snake Charmer: "Did Rob tell you to move?"

Me: "Nope."

Snake Charmer: "Your telling me Rob gave you no moving money at all."

Me: "Yep"

Snake Charmer: "Hmm, Rob tells me he gave you cash in Florida."

Me: "Absolutely no, no. A thousand times no." (I knew this was coming)

Snake Charmer: (pause) Ahem, "Well there seems to be a mix up here, let me get back to you later, goodbye."

Me: "Bye."

Now I know what has happened. Rob told his boss the Snake Charmer that I received the money, while ol' Rob played Santa Claus that Christmas with my moving money. Holy hell, another mess! I was ready for this one, I knew what would happen next. As soon as I called in for messages Rob would be on that phone pleading with me to say that I received the money for future privileges from him. I called in and right on schedule;

Rob:"Hey pardner, how are you doing?"
Me: "Not bad, how are you?"
Rob: "Hey pardner, you got to get my grapes out of the fire!
Me: "How can I do that?"
Rob: "Tell Baker that I gave you cash in Florida, $1800 of it!
Me: "Rob, let me get this straight, you want me to lie for you and jeopardize myself (interrupt)
Rob: "No pardner, not lie just give me time to get the cash together".
Me: "Rob, I wouldn't lie for my brother about this much less for you.
Rob: "I'LL FIRE YOU!
Me: "Go ahead."
Rob: "I will"...dial tone.

Now he has to prove I had the money, which I didn't. He has to be scuffling now going to Baker to plead his case. But I am sure Baker will be trying to save his own ass by doing a little scuffling on his own. He was...He scuffled his way down to "Our Big Guy".

OBG: "Bill, how are you?"
Me: "Fine, how are you?"
OBG: "Bill why didn't you move to Pittsburgh? I thought you were already there".
Me: "I never received any moving money from Rob".
OBG: "None?"
Me: "Nope."

OBG: "Well this has to be looked into further. I will be back to you, hang in . there, so long".
Me: "Talk to you later."

Now the stage is set. Obviously Rob spent the buckaroos, as I thought, and didn't have it. The Snake Charmer knew that and couldn't cover anymore. So he bailed out to the Big Guy and was letting Rob go adrift. There was nothing I could do but wait, and wait I did.

For two days when Rob called again;

Rob (much more subdued): "Hey pardner, here's what I need, you take momma to Pittsburgh stay in the best hotels, feed her the best and please find an apartment and get a mover and I'll fly out to give the mover the money. I need a receipt from a mover to save my tail, O.K. pardner, O.K.?
Me: I agree, because deep down I like Rob, and as long as he pays the mover I could care less. Now to talk the Little Woman into this folly. I know we will never move to Pittsburgh. How can I make the Little Woman believe this?

Again, I'm following my gut and my gut says this exercise will never come to pass. Finally after two days I convince the Little Woman to go. We go through this mental masturbation, as I know, as sure as I know my name and the pervert's, we will never move to the once smoky city.

National Company is paying the tab for this folly and momma is somewhat enjoying it. We finally put a deposit on an apartment in Pittsburgh and back home we go. We now have an address and a receipt for $100. Now to find a mover. I go through the yellow pages and back to Moving Man for an estimate. Moving Man gives me an estimate of $1464.00 sealed and delivered. I call Rob to inform him of my success and he is ecstatic, he makes wanton promises about how he will take care of my ass for this act of kindness for the rest of my natural life.

He states he will be here April fourteenth, to pay Mr. Mover and for me to meet him in Philadelphia at ten a.m. He arrives and I go pick him up and drive back home. The conversation on the way home was interesting to say the least. Rob tells me he can levitate, also reads minds and hates women. I deposit Rob at the Holiday Inn with him insisting that he can lift my car off the ground, just by willing it. This guy has turned into a real banana. I've had enough of him and tell him so and as of all people of his ilk, he responds by stammering something inaudible.   Our appointment with Mr. Mover is at ten the next morning so I bid Rob ado. I'll meet him at ten and I tell him to have his check ready. He says he will and I say goodbye.

I know I am in trouble when Rob tries to borrow ten dollars from me for breakfast. Now here is a fellow who's job is on the line for a moving receipt of $1500.00 and he is borrowing ten dollars from me. I was born forty-three years ago, so I know that Rob is going to bounce this check on the mover, unless it is certified.

I now know, as we are to face to face with Mr. Mover that the latter is not so. Rob suggests that he will write the check out to me, I then should deposit it in my account. Then in turn I should write Mr. Mover a check. Wow! This guy is a beaut. I halt this conversation by excusing us from Mr. Mover and go outside to set Rob straight. I tell Rob at this point I wouldn't accept his check; also I wouldn't touch his check with a ten-foot pole. If he wants that all saving moving receipt, he better write Mr. Mover a check and get that errant money in his account pronto. Rob stares and almost confesses, but he doesn't, and with the biggest pair of brass balls that I've seen in a long time, he writes a rubber check for one thousand four hundred sixty dollars and seventy-two cents. Mr. Mover accepts, and hands Rob his saving grace, the receipt.

Now I know I'm a witness to a bizarre act. What do I do? I have two options:

Shut up and don't move.

Call our "Big Guy".

Call the Snake Charmer.

Shut up and let nature take its course.

I choose to shut up and let nature take its course. What debauchery, it is never ending. I go home pray for guidance, self-control and peace.

There is an industrial show in Detroit, Michigan and I hop a plane to attend. I'm met by Lookingood at the airport and he relates a story of how last night he was in one of Detroit's finest discos. He is approached at the bar by some lovely and she just fell all over him until her escort himself showed up to beg his wayward misses back. Where is the sanity? At every turn I'm involved with liars thieves and clodhoppers. The show is uneventful with the exception of getting paged at the Joe Louis Arena by National Company's lawyer and the message reads to call him. It is more questions about Rob and Lou Briskett, a troublemaker himself, Lou has thrown dispersion back to Rob. I was acquainted with both of these lads, and Company lawyer wants to know what I knew. As stated I told the truth, the whole truth and nothing but the truth, so help me God.

The flight from Detroit to home was right on schedule, with the Little Woman waiting for me at the terminal. I noticed as I took her hand she seemed to have something to tell me. She did. Mr. Mover had called two hours ago and you guessed it, Rob's personal check bounced. Mr. Mover had called Rob but could not reach him. I will call Rob as soon as bag and baggage are secured.

Bag and baggage are secured, thrown in the trunk of the car and homeward bound we are. A new computer service had been installed at our local airport so it is much easier to play gypsy.

At home at last, I rush to the phone to call my wayward boss. Finally he is on the line and states it was just a big ol mix up pardner. Everything is all taken care of. Of course I believe none of this, as he is putting a little pressure on me to move as soon as possible. I will hear none of this, I state, "that until Mr. Mover has a check that will clear Rob's bank not by bouncing over it either". We say our byes and I call Mr. Mover to see if he has the check, he said yes, and I say hold on I'll be right over. I am on Mr. Mover's loading dock before he could say cancelled check. I ask if it is possible to Xerox Rob boys check. Mr. Movers says alright no skin off my ass. Mr. Mover copies it and off I am with the spongy paper. I noticed in the box checked on the back of the check "insufficient funds" is noted. I also noted the check had been put through twice. This tells me Rob has no intentions of making this check or any check any good. I arrive home and the Little Woman says to call Mr. Mover again. I do. He says Rob called and is sending another check. While sending this check he wants Mr. Mover to return the adjusted one, as Rob calls it. Mr. Mover replied, no. If and when he receives a good check, he will do just that. Rob tries again, but Mr. Mover is steadfast, so Rob backs off saying the check is in the mail today and it should be there on Friday, as this is Monday.

Mr. Mover calls early Friday stating the check has arrived and what to do? Hold on I'm coming over and we are going to the bank together to cash it. I might as well be right there, it will be easier to Xerox it at the bank. We wait as it is drawn on a California bank, and it takes one and a half hours to respond by computer. The hour and a half wait is as long is it taken for the check to bounce three thousand miles back. No funds, zero, zilch, zip, notta. Nothing in the old bankerino in Orange California.

I call Rob's secretary, who happens to be my secretary also, Rob is not in but he has dictated a memo to the Snake Charmer before he left, and beautiful Carlotta states the memo doesn't look kosher to her. She is very bright and has had enough of "pardner's" shenanigans. She states she will send me a copy of the memo, Federal Express. As I'm not copied on the memo, I thank her a lot and she says it should be there on Saturday. Mucho Gracias Carlotta. Now just sit and wait until tomorrow. Federal Express arrives early the next day and I read the memo, as it is a beaut.

Here goes;

Inner office memo from: Rob
To: Mr. Baker
Subject: Mr. Barna's moving money

I feel it is in the best interest for all concerned in discern of Mr. Barna's moving at this time. The reason for this action simply stated is that Mr. Barna's mental state at this time can be best described as shaky. I personally feel in this mental state it should also be considered to release Mr. Barna of his employ. As I have decided to stop payment on the check for moving expenses. Any questions do not hesitate to call me.

Sincerely Yours,
Rob

Now is that beautiful or what? This Son of a Bitch that I have tried to help along has really turned the screw to save his butt. He is almost right about one thing though, my mental state. Only I wouldn't describe it as shaky, a better word would be crazed.

Since it is Saturday I will have to wait until Monday to call our "Big Guy" and drop my ace in the hole in his lap and try to get ol Rob bounced like the two copies of the bounced checks I'm holding.

At exactly eleven AM on Monday EST, I'm calling our "Big Guy", I'm livid but composed and logical.

Me: "Hello, Our Big Guy this is Bill Barna"
OBG: "Hi ya Bill, what can I do for you?"
Me: "Concerning this memo Rob sent around, I would like to clear this pack of lies up".
OBG: "Shoot, I was wondering what this was all about>"
Me: "Well for one he bounced two checks on the mover and I'm holding copies of both. Number two, as for my mental state he is correct but it has been created by all of his nonsense that I won't get into at this time but call on me for a full report".
OBG: "Bill, send me, if you would, those copies Federal Express ASAP."
Me: "Will do."
OBG: "Hang in there, I'll be calling you."
Me: "O.K."
OBG: "See you."
Me: "Bye."

Our Big Guy almost sounds sincere in his conversation with me. I feel somewhat better knowing that at least ol Rob is being summoned at this moment to our "Big Guys" sanctum to explain his shenanigans that are contained in the purple and white envelope that has just started its twenty-four hour journey to the land of fun and sun. Magically as much turmoil that has been created in the last time frame of which without it, this book would not have been written is now ebbing.

It seems Rob cannot maneuver out of this debauchery and he is relieved of his duties ASAP. Our "Big Guy" calls to comfort me in my hour of need. He also lets me know that he thinks that I am solid morally and spiritually. Our "Big Guy" also apologizes all over the watts line to my wife and me for all of the aggravation that National Company has caused us. Our "Big Guy" is also sending us a monetary sum to alleviate our anxieties and aggravation. All of this comes forth without me even asking. What all of this tells me is that I must have a good case for a lawsuit. But being the solid moral and Spiritual guy he claims I have become now, I ask you how could I sue them?

I have been trying to figure out how to end these scribblings for about one and a half years. Unfortunately so many more things have happened in that time, that could keep me rambling on, but I have become mentally lazy and I don't need therapy anymore. This book saved my sanity or what was left of it. Everyone should write all of their, or part of their lives in a novel form as I did. It is truly great therapy that is unmatched anywhere. If there are any "shrinks" shrinking as they read this, I would appreciate your comments, not that they would be taken seriously but I would appreciate them all the same.

Our state of affairs at this point could be better, they could also be worse. The Little Woman is secure in her life having most of our siblings grown and out she is constantly keeping busy with different endeavors. The latest being piano lessons.

Daughter number one is flying the friendly skies as a stewardess with a major airline. She appears to be moving in a positive direction, realizing her dream as a flight attendant, traveling the globe and loving it. It appears in the few times that I see her there are murmurings between her and the Little Woman, of a serious romance budding, between her and a Norseman pilot. I think his name is Addalot, or something like that, for as always I am not privy to the details. It seems that daughter number one is excited about this and he could be the one. I haven't met him yet, as daughter number one is putting this off. This tells me that this is serious, as she is protecting him from me. All I can say is, if this boy is going to nuptuate daughter number one, he better be tough, we will see what happens, it shall be very interesting. She is truly amazing that girl, don't tell her but I do admire her. She is a real piece of work. She stopped by today sporting a shiner from a fall on a slippery floor. I think it looks cute. Maybe I'll get the scoop today.

Daughter number two is running a medical unit in Doylestown, Pennsylvania. She also has a following of males, but she is very discreet with her guys. So I can't relate any information on these guys. My relationship with her could be better. I feel the move to the land of fruits and nuts hurt her more than the rest, but if she reads this, I have one thing to say to you. "I love you", and I am truly sorry for all of the pain you experienced.

Daughter number three is fine. She is getting ready to go to the New Jersey shore to live and work on the boardwalk this summer. She also is continuing her vocation in her self-education as a nurse recommending various solutions to the minor ills that we encounter everyday, for she without any formal education is very accurate in her diagnosis. And her passion for this is only exceeded by her beauty and brains. She will be starting college in the fall and then continue her pursuit of being a nurse. I am sure she will be an excellent nurse as I am hoping to call on her when my body doesn't rally to my commands for healing as middle age and worse comes to pay a house call.

Number one son has turned into a six foot good looking, doing lousy in school type of guy. At fifteen he's looking forward to "cruising and scoping chicks". He is also trying to amass car insurance money by carrying papers, washing cars and begging money from me. He is the apple that didn't fall far from the tree. Number one son is also a self-proclaimed "scoring machine".

With that I will tell you of my status, I have more lines and less hair, life is unfair. Boils grow back, tonsils grow back, tumors grow back, etc. Things like limbs and hair that you might like to have back, won't. My hair used to blow around in the wind, now my neck does. I am still with National Company, with a few new bosses in the interim. My sanity has returned (I am glad that grew back). I am looking forward to really accomplishing something in the next half of my life. Probably like existing with a minimum of aggravation. What can one say when one has said all one can say, I guess The End?

P.S. Buy two they are small!

THE END

Epilogue

A new day is dawning as I am reading an article in the local newspaper over coffee, cigarettes and my water. It seems a fellow of small stature has been accidentally killed on a city street. It seems this fellow was crossing the street against the light, when a beer truck driven by a lady named Ima A. Nympfo, of sixty-nine Never Satisfied Lane of the city, flattened him. As it appears his shoestring came loose on his red P.F. sneakers. He, stopped to tie the errant lace, was then hit in the middle of the street. Miss Nympfo, according to the article, states that because of his size and his crouching to tie his sneaker he could not be seen very well, as it was snowing. Miss Nympfo was very upset as the article states and was much beside herself. The scene obviously was a grim one, as it went on to describe how the Homburg, that he was wearing was also flattened by the crash! As my mind is clearing after coffee and cigarettes, it seems this fellow is starting to become familiar to me. Could this be, could this be, my nemesis Worse, who has caused me untold misery and woe. I refer quickly to the last of the article by passing the verbiage of a pinky ring and sweatshirt described as all that was left. There was no identification found, but it seems a short fellow claimed the remains, telling the authorities that he was his only surviving son...

Printed in the United States
63248LVS00002B/85-102